Dear Mystery Lover,

The Seventh Sacrament introduces a fresh new voice and protagonist to the mystery field. James Bradberry is an award-winning architect who has taught his craft at Yale, the University of Pennsylvania and Temple University. But Jim also loves to write and DEAD LETTER is very happy that he has found the time to create his alter ego, Jamie Ramsgill.

Who's killing the world's great architects? Ramsgill, a professor of architecture and amateur sleuth, is determined to find out. Full of the detail and insight that only a professional architect can bring to the table, *The Seventh Sacrament* takes the reader into a whole new world, where sparring egos and a high-stakes competition bring out the best and the worst in one of the most creative of professions.

Look for Jim's next Jamie Ramsgill mystery, *Ruins of Civility*, in hardcover from St. Martin's Press in January 1996. This time Jamie is at Oxford, England, but the stakes are just as high.

Keep your eye out for DEAD LETTER—and build yourself a library of paperback mysteries to die for.

Yours in crime,

Shawn Coyne
Senior Editor
St. Martin's DEAD LETTER Paperback Mysteries

Titles now available from St. Martin's Dead Letter Mysteries

PRAISE FOR *THE SEVENTH SACRAMENT*

"An old-fashioned mystery in gleaming new dress . . . Bradberry satirizes his profession's star system and ever-changing fashions and keeps readers guessing . . . An ingenious twist at the end."
                    —*Publishers Weekly* (starred review)

"The lush Italian setting is lovingly described with an eye for detail, the style is elegant and the author's erudition evident."
                    —*Poisoned Pen*

"Writing rich with the language of architecture and the flavor of Italy. An amusing look into a professional world. Well-written and thoughtfully plotted—with a pleasingly surprising ending."
                    —*Kirkus Reviews*

"Plenty of color and detail, odd characters, and a 'whodunit' with precise architectural detail."
                    —*Lake Oswego Review*

"A stylish, entertaining debut. Along with a lush setting and quirky, vivid characters, James Bradberry even succeeds in making architecture sexy."
    —Les Roberts, author of *The Lemon Chicken Jones*

"A book of intelligence and erudition . . . Drenched in atmosphere and rich in setting . . . The plot is satisfying in the same manner as a well-designed building."
                    —Neil Albert, author of *The January Corpse*

St. Martin's Paperbacks by James Bradberry

THE SEVENTH SACRAMENT

*Coming in hardcover from St. Martin's Press
in January 1996*

RUINS OF CIVILITY

THE
SEVENTH
SACRAMENT

JAMES BRADBERRY

St. Martin's Paperbacks

THE SEVENTH SACRAMENT

Copyright © 1994 by James Bradberry

Library of Congress Catalog Card Number: 94-2836

ISBN: 0-312-95636-3

Printed in the United States of America

St. Martin's Press hardcover edition/July 1994
St. Martin's Paperbacks edition/November 1995

10 9 8 7 6 5 4 3 2 1

For Nancy

Acknowledgments

My heartfelt thanks to the following people: Blanche Schlessinger, my agent, for her sound guidance and ceaseless encouragement; Michael Denneny and (especially) John Clark of St. Martin's Press for their thoughtful suggestions and patience with a neophyte; Dr. Dimitri Contostavolos, Medical Examiner of Delaware County, Pennsylvania, for advice in a realm far beyond my own; and Louisa and Philippa, my daughters, whose crayonwork on a multitude of discarded manuscript pages brought color and joy into the black-and-white world of rewrites.

THE
SEVENTH
SACRAMENT

ONE

A light rain drifted out of the sky as the plane touched down in Verona. The August heat was stifling, but as we drove northwest and approached Lake Garda, the air cooled, the sky blued, and my mind drifted back to my year in Italy. It had been almost two decades since my fellowship in Venice, but driving on these twisting roads, lined by tall dark cypresses and picturesque villages of pastel stucco, all illuminated in that orange Mediterranean light, northern Italy seemed as familiar to me now as cycling past Nassau Hall on the way to the architecture school had just two days ago.

But this drive differed. Eighteen years ago I wouldn't have been traveling in a chauffeur-driven Bentley, heading towards the Renaissance villa of Dottor Renzo Piruzzi, accompanied by two of the foremost architects in the world. And I certainly wouldn't have been receiving two thousand dollars a day from Piruzzi, Italy's premier manufacturer of avant-garde designer furniture and one of the wealthiest men in the world, for my services as advisor to an architectural competition that was about to take place at the villa. The competition would involve the world's most renowned architects, but at this point I knew only a few of the details.

But even university professors sometimes have adventure in life, and the letter that I and the participants had received just two weeks earlier outlined an architectural contest that had piqued everyone's interest. Six architects—two American, one British, one French, one Italian and one Japanese—would compete to design Piruzzi S.p.A.'s new world headquarters outside Milan. The winner of the competition, which was to be judged solely by Dottor Piruzzi, would be awarded a commission for the building, with an estimated fee of five million dollars. A more than adequate reward for a weekend's worth of work.

The letter went on to state that Piruzzi had no architectural predilections, that he would give no hint of a program for the building, and that each architect would be on his or her own—given forty-eight hours, reference and drafting materials, sustenance and accommodation, to come up with the winning design. At the end of the weekend, each would present a sketch design to our host, including plans, elevations and a model.

The only hitch was this: designing architecture is a labor-intensive endeavor. The design of such a large and complex building, and the preparation of drawings to illustrate it, would normally take a team of architects and engineers weeks, if not months, to produce. In this case, however, the six architects, all middle- to late-middle-aged, would each be required to do the entire project alone, in physical and intellectual isolation. All during their weekend stay. No young designers from their offices to work with them. No draftsmen. No engineers. No help whatsoever. Solo competitors, like a college entrance examination. The prize was immense, and I was euphoric, as though the six great designers were to be my students for the weekend. However, my euphoria was to be short-lived.

We turned onto a narrow street off of Salò's lakefront piazza and wound our way up to the edge of town. Tall houses yielded to chalky hillside orchards, and as the steepness of the hills increased, the thin ribbon of shell-encrusted asphalt on which we were traveling veered to find a suitable grade. We climbed a few thousand feet, leaving farms and settlements behind us. Straight stretches of road became less frequent, and with each switchback, the brilliant blue basin of Lake Garda below us faded further into the atmospheric haze. We soon entered a dense but stunted forest, and as we emerged from it the villa gates came into view.

Beyond the gates the Villa Piruzzi unfolded as a building of stunning architectural beauty. Formal yet sprawling, in the cinquecento style, warm pitted stone stained by the weather of four and a half centuries, it reached out and embraced us, eliciting a collective sigh.

"My God," said my friend Richard Battle, sitting in the front seat of the sedan. He had slept most of the way from Verona and was just now waking up. "Am I in a dream?"

"So I awoke, and behold it was a dream," said Sir Colin Garbutt, to my left. "The Blenheim Palace, with panache."

I laughed to myself, thinking of how the British always seem to belittle their own architectural legacy. But *panache* was the right word for what stood before us, a scene done up in a way only the Italians know how to do.

The villa rested upon a broad plateau, at the end of a great flat axis. The axis was a drive of radiant white, formed of crushed marble chips. It was lined on both sides by a parade of potted topiaries, bold evergreens sculpted into cones and spheres, each separated from its neighbor by a crisp line of low impenetrable hedge. Beyond the hedge, a carpeted lawn incised in a perfect patchwork of light and dark green stretched out to meet the dependent wings of the villa, great encapsulating arms, fronted by arched colonnades. The whole was dominated by the middle, the main house, a three-story cube that terminated the drive. It was a crescendo unto itself, its manneristic energy focused inward, its superimposed architectural orders like some great scrambled set of building blocks, all old, all geometric, all brought alive by the noonday sun. Marble figures danced atop the attic, teetering above the heavy balustrade that capped the denticulated cornice. Finely proportioned windows appeared as little houses across the broad stucco facade, each with its own entablature and pediment. The base of the building was enveloped by a heavy rustication of stone, through which five graceful archways had been cut to form a front porch.

We parked beside a circular fountain, baroque in design, which was hovered over by a collection of cavorting marble nymphs. The car was immediately set upon by several servants in livery who emptied the trunk of our baggage and disappeared into the house. I got out and stretched, filling my lungs with mountain air.

"Buon giorno!"

A large man scurried towards us from the house. He had a broad round face, bronzed and shining, on which a stubby black moustache held sway. His small ears turned out at their tops, and lined up with eyes the color of beluga caviar. A dimpled chin was surrounded by puffy cheeks—it seemed the vestige of a younger thinner face. He wore a tangerine blazer with bright brass buttons, white slacks and socks, and thin loafers of supple cowhide that covered the smallest feet I have ever seen on an adult. He reeked of wealth.

"Welcome."

Garbutt extended his hand. "Dottor Piruzzi. I'm Colin Garbutt."

"Oh, I know, sir." He gave Garbutt an embrace in the Italian manner, patting him across the shoulder blades with soft manicured fingers that were ringed in gold. "And you . . . you must be the American, Battle."

Richard Battle embraced the Italian and managed a smile, though I couldn't tell if his lukewarm reaction was because he had just woken up, or because he didn't appreciate being referred to by only his last name.

Piruzzi then turned to me. He paused and shot me a

short inquisitive glance before saying:

"Are you Professor Ramsgill?" His voice had an incredulous tone to it, as if what he meant to ask was, "You couldn't *possibly* be Professor Ramsgill, could you?"

I suppose his surprise was a reaction to my boyish face, a reaction that I'd have to say I often get. Though I don't consider someone in their late thirties to be particularly young, I *looked* young compared to the other architects who were to be at the villa, being at least fifteen years their junior.

"Please call me Jamie, er . . . ," I said, not quite sure how to address him. *Dottore* was an honorary title, and I was uncertain of the protocol.

"And myself . . . Renzo." He looked me in the eye but a fraction of a second before turning away. He rested his hand on Battle's shoulder, and the three older men walked ahead as I followed them inside.

We passed through a lofty marble foyer, the sound of our heels resounding upon the polished stone like a loud fluttering of wings. We descended a flight of polychrome terrazzo stairs and arrived at a great dining hall. It was rich in ornament and cluttered with antiques, and light filtered in from tall deep-silled windows draped in gold silk.

"Ladies and gentlemen," Piruzzi said, "let me introduce everyone."

Three men and a woman stood before us around a buffet table. One of the men was dressed in a tuxedo, and he was younger than the others. He was introduced as Franco Cavalliere, head of household for Dottor Piruzzi. The others I had met before, at lectures or other functions, and I knew the work of each of them exceedingly well.

First there was Pet Clissac. Parisian, educated at Bordeaux, holder of the Légion d'honneur. As a woman, an anomaly in a profession that has a decidedly male-dominated star system, her reputation was based upon her writings and only a few highly theoretical projects, inspirational to a whole generation of younger architects. She was a small woman, with dusty blond hair on its way towards gray. Her piercing eyes were set close beneath a high, grooved forehead, and though it wasn't a kind thought, her face reminded me of that of a mole. She held a brown cigarette in the Continental fashion and exhaled with tight lips directed up at the ceiling. She seemed indifferent to her introduction, and I got the feeling that she was more comfortable in the studio or the library than in a conversation with other humans.

The second of the architects was Akio Hara. Hara was head of the architecture school at Tokyo University, and he had a sizable practice on the side. He was a short man dressed in a somewhat baggy teal-colored suit. He had an angular face with bulging dark green eyes, black hair combed over wet to smallish ears. His glistening white smile dominated his other features. He was younger than Clissac—I put him in his late fifties—and as he was introduced to each of us, he bowed and presented his business card. I was embarrassed not to be able to give him one of my own (I could never remember to keep the damn things), and I made a mental note to replenish my supply once I got back to the States.

Third was Thornburgh Keller of New York, dean of American architects, about whose work I was indifferent. He represented everything I don't like about our profession, most notably how the old-boy network can make a superstar out of a mediocre talent. He was in his late sixties, a product of Penn, long a champion of the Modern movement until it became more prudent to adopt Post-Modernism. In recent years he had done a one-eighty again, this time to Deconstructivism. Nevertheless his apostasy had not denied him a Pritzker Prize, architecture's equivalent to the Nobel. He was turned out as if for the boardroom—blue Savile Row pinstripes, knotted gold cuff links, short white hair and eyeglasses with heavy brown frames. The lenses of his eyeglasses were thick and his eyes weak with age, but his face had a warmth to it and his voice and elocution were without flaw.

Sir Colin Garbutt, from London, was the oldest of the competition participants. Debrett's put his age at seventy-two, but I had my suspicions. His long and distinguished career began after Cambridge, and his most notable designs were for the Office of Foreign Affairs and other Whitehall buildings. His face seemed the epitome of a British country gentleman—ruddy skin, protruding jaw, wavy white locks, spiraling eyebrows. He was a big man and his features were matched by his clothing, tweeds upon suede with a dash of plaid, all of which made him appear more ready for a weekend foxhunt than for what was about to transpire.

And finally, Richard Battle of Philadelphia, someone whom I had known for years. He had once taught with me at Princeton, and there we had forged a friendship based on mutual beliefs, though in recent years we had drifted apart. Richard was tall and very slender, with a rounded gray-brown beard. His head hung forward, beyond his center of gravity, which somehow made him look unstable. He was a casual dresser, today in a cable knit sweater and unpressed khaki trousers, scuffed loafers and loud red socks. His dress defied his manner, which, as an architect anyway, tended toward perfectionism. He was a Yale man, and his considerable talent was matched with an exceedingly calm personality, which lately, as his practice had waned, had transformed into sullenness. He recently confided in me that he was tired of big commissions and that at his age—sixty-two—he enjoyed the residential projects and other smaller jobs he was getting. I'd have to admit that I didn't believe him. After all, he had accepted the *dottore*'s invitation to design an enormous project, and were he to win the competition, he would have to build his office back up to a respectable size.

"Aren't we missing someone?" I asked Piruzzi after the

introductions. Piruzzi was pouring wine for my friend
Battle, who had been eyeing the bar.

"Yes. Gio Borromini," Piruzzi said. "He telephoned
this morning, and unfortunately he's been detained in
Rome. He'll join us this evening. Now," he said, changing the subject, "we should eat. The food is prepared."

Was it ever. We were led to an outdoor terrace and a
long table covered in white linen, overflowing with a
sumptuous meal. We sat beneath canvas umbrellas while
a cool breeze worked its way up the mountainside, gently
blowing the aroma of olives, melon, cheese and *bresaola*
under our noses. I placed myself between the Englishman
Garbutt and the Japanese Hara, and quickly rummaged
my mind for talk that might be of interest to them.

"Extraordinary, don't you think . . . young Ramsgill?"

Garbutt was looking beyond a balustrade of worn
stone. The landscape was verdant and almost tropical—
palms, bananas, hibiscuses, and flowering vines mixed in
with the cypress and pine. The land fell off sharply, and
far below us were the orange terra-cotta roofs of Salò
and the deep blue lake. Beyond the lake, mountains rose
as flat as a picture in a postcard.

"It's paradise," I said. "How do these plants survive
this close to the Alps?"

Garbutt was delicately chewing an olive.

"Somehow protected, you know, from the wind and
like that. Don't really understand it. We British have
been coming here forever. Discovered it on our Italian
grand tours of the eighteenth century."

Hara nodded politely.

"Hmh," said Pet Clissac. She was putting out a cigarette across the table. "The Gauls were in this area in the
fourth century."

"How's that?" Garbutt asked, cupping a hand to his
ear. Having driven from Verona with him, I'd learned
that his hearing was bad.

"We were here long before the British," Clissac said
loudly.

"Ah, but you didn't stay, now did you, my dear?"

Clissac sent a piercing gaze towards the old man's head. France and Britain as chauvinistic as ever, I thought, but then I remembered a recent attack on Sir Colin's work delivered by Clissac in *L'Architecture d'aujourd'hui,* a French journal. Brutal would be too kind a word for what she had written. She had called Garbutt's Office of Foreign Affairs something like "Miesian necrophilia," in reference to Garbutt's emulation of the designs of the late Modern master Ludwig Mies van der Rohe. She likened Sir Colin's compositional skills to those of the dung beetle, and even from the sardonic mind of a French intellectual, that could hardly be taken as a compliment. I don't recall a response from Garbutt, but it did come back to me now that Piruzzi, in one of his preliminary letters to me last year, had asked me how I thought Clissac and Garbutt might get along. I think I responded at the time that it certainly could be no worse than Clissac and Battle, who were bitter enemies, though at that point both had already been selected to compete. As a matter of fact, it now came to mind that with the exception of Hara, who was a perfect Japanese gentleman, all of the participants, including Borromini, had at one time or another had their professional spats.

I was thinking this as my eyes shifted to Piruzzi, reigning at the head of the table, not talking, but sipping wine and watching his competitors converse. He seemed to be enjoying it, and it occurred to me at that moment that he was either a sadist for putting together such a group, or incredibly shrewd. I sat back and savored my own wine, which was an excellent Barolo, probably one of the recent greats from the late seventies. Unlike most competitions I was familiar with, in which a commission and one or two prizes are awarded, Piruzzi had in this case guaranteed a cash prize for each of the architects who didn't win. On a descending scale from several thousand dollars for second place, each succeeding place would be awarded a lesser amount. Sixth prize was to be the equivalent of a few hundred U.S. dollars. A humiliating offer. And because of that, each architect would be ranked from first to last. Knowing the stature of the people around the table, the ego required to rise to the top of a profession in which the artistic endeavor involves millions of dollars, no one, and I mean no one, at that table, now that they had accepted the *dottore*'s invitation, would allow themselves to finish at the bottom of the heap. I was in awe. It was a devilish plan.

TWO

Lunch lingered, and shortly after two we left Piruzzi to some business and were shown the villa by Franco Cavalliere. The tour confirmed my first impressions of the place, and I was particularly taken by the beautiful gardens. We made our way through them all: parterre gardens formed of boxwoods and annual beds, dense allées of ancient cypresses punctuated by rococo nymphaea, an alpine rock garden that hugged the mountain-side with heather and exotic Himalayan plants. Finally we returned to the area of the dining room and emerged into the finest landscape of all, a courtyard garden of unique design.

It was constructed around a bosk of pleached olive trees, their jagged branches like a multitude of arthritic fingers reaching towards the sky. The tree trunks were clothed neatly in helix ivy. The floor of the garden was made of Belgian block, in the radial pattern known as Roman cobbles. The garden itself was a play of green texture—billowy and formal, light and dark, exotic and commonplace. Deep recesses and exedrae played against the sunlit trees. In one of the trees, hardly visible among the cool foliage, rested an albino peacock. Other unpigmented peafowl milled about, their white surfaces etched by dappled light, sharp rustling sounds spreading through the garden each time one of the males unfurled its tail feathers.

The entire garden was built upon a high terrace that jutted out from the mountain. It was enclosed by an arched colonnade of Roman brick and travertine. The colonnade linked a group of unusual pavilions, seven of them in all. Each was two stories tall with a classical portico, but all were different. The three primary orders were used, Doric, Ionic and Corinthian, as well as Tuscan and Composite variations. The pavilions flanked the garden three to a side, and at the end of the garden, on an axis away from the house, was a slightly larger pavilion that seemed to hold some importance over the others. It was a bizarre combination of classical and Egyptian motifs, topped by a roof in the form of an Egyptian pyramid, and upon the pyramid, carved out of marble, a dove with a spike through its heart.

"Each of you will occupy a single pavilion," said Piruzzi's majordomo.

"Which of us goes where?" asked Richard Battle, his voice warm and rhythmic from wine.

"Professor Ramsgill will reside in the big pavilion. In a moment I'll show each of the rest of you to the pavilion you are to occupy. Each is exactly the same inside. You will find a bedroom on the ground floor, an adjoining bath and balcony. On the upper floor is a studio. Each pavilion has all of your needs, including a phone. The phone is for internal communication and doesn't reach outside the villa. When you're working, you'll not leave your quarters. If you have questions about the competition, call for Ramsgill. If you have any other needs, call me."

Battle and I exchanged glances. Except for the oddness of the Egypto-Roman pavilion, I was flattered by my status in the hierarchy. I could tell everyone back home that for one brief weekend, at least, I had reigned over the great designers of the world. Then I remembered, of course, that unlike the others, I had no hope of winning

the multimillion-dollar commission. So much for my exalted perch.

We each were then directed to our separate quarters.
My pavilion was simple inside, with whitewashed walls
and beamed ceilings, furniture in the painted Venetian
style. My bedroom was upstairs, and in it my clothes had
been unpacked and put away. Above the bed was a crucifix of bronze.

I washed my face and changed shirts, then stepped out
onto my balcony. As the garden was built upon the terrace, its back side was formed by rampart-like walls rising out of the hill. Each pavilion was separated from its
neighbor by about the length of two rooms. Below me
was a dense wooded hillside painted in pools of warm
light, and beyond that in the distance, Salò and the lake.
My pavilion had a balcony that stretched from one side
of the pavilion to the other. From its south side I could
see three of my neighbors, and from the north side three
more. The other pavilions had balconies too, and as I
stood upon mine, one by one the other architects stepped
out, waved and returned inside.

I pulled a spiral-bound sketchbook from my briefcase
and noted in a drawing the plan of our quarters and
where each of the competitors was staying. My sketch-
books serve as visual diaries, and I've been keeping them
since my first trip abroad, over two decades ago.

My pavilion was farthest from the main house. To my
left, next door, was New York's Thornburgh Keller.
Next to him was to be Gio Borromini and closest to the
house, Sir Colin Garbutt. Nearest to me on the other side
was the Frenchwoman Pet Clissac. Beyond her was the
Japanese, Hara, and up near the house, Battle. I pondered for a moment Piruzzi's purpose in placing each as
he had done. I couldn't think of a reason, but I knew in
the back of my mind that there must be one. Piruzzi had
thought of every detail.

I was about to return to the garden when something
caught my eye. It was a note of red below me in the near

distance amongst the lush green growth, a woman in a scarlet dress poised at the edge of a footpath with a portable video camera aimed into the trees. I couldn't imagine what she was recording, then I paused, and for the first time noticed a beautiful chorus of bird songs filtering through the woods. It was as if the trees themselves were singing, the entire wood alive with music. I stood for a moment listening, wondering who the woman was, then almost as suddenly as she had appeared, she was gone.

I returned to the garden, where several of the architects were talking with Cavalliere.

"Who built it?" asked Sir Colin, referring to the villa.

"An ancestor of the *dottore*'s," said Cavalliere. "In the sixteenth century. His name was Andrea Braegno. A papal emissary to one of the Chigis, or Medicis . . . oh, I don't remember which. He was one of the Orsinis. A very powerful family to this part of the country. This was his summer villa."

"What's the history of this particular garden . . . and the pavilions?" Thornburgh Keller asked.

"For Braegno, as for the *dottore* . . . guest quarters, I suppose."

Richard Battle scowled. "No way," he said. "There would've been a higher purpose. A Renaissance mind wouldn't've settled on such a temporal plane."

"Well then, Richard, enlighten us. A higher purpose such as . . . ?" said Thornburgh Keller.

Battle hesitated. It was as if he wanted to keep some confidential information to himself.

"A higher purpose such as educating," he finally said, looking Keller straight in the eye. "Unlike what's in today's magazines, there was a time, Thornburgh, when architecture carried deep meaning."

Which was a slightly veiled way of saying that Keller's work carried less than deep meaning, because Keller's designs were always featured in the magazines.

Keller returned the volley: "At least some people have

enough work to get in the magazines," he said.

The two of them stared at one another in silence.

"Then what *would* be the meaning of the garden, Richard?" I asked.

He was looking around the group of us, his eyes now flitting like a cornered animal.

"The garden opens off a sequence of rooms in the big house, right?" he said. "The closest room to the garden is the dining room. And the garden is represented symmetrically by seven pavilions."

"So?"

"So then it's quite simple. The seven pavilions represent the seven planets, just as murals in the dining room represent the heavens."

I hadn't noticed the murals.

"Why do you say that?" asked Pet Clissac, who had just joined us. "Last time I checked there were nine planets in the solar system."

Again Battle frowned.

"In the fifteenth century," he said. "Man knew of seven celestial bodies. There was the Sun and Moon of course, then Venus and Mars. As well as Jupiter, Mercury and Saturn."

Hara and Cavalliere seemed impressed by Battle's knowledge. Clissac shrank back defensively, as if she'd been slapped.

"Could be planets," I said a moment later. "But Richard, really, the planets don't exactly have a lock on the number seven in Renaissance symbolism. Take religion, for instance. There are the seven sorrows of the Virgin, the seven deadly sins, the seven churches of Rome, and probably a lot of other sevens I can't even remember."

Richard started to speak but was interrupted by Clissac.

"Or the seven liberal arts, *mon ami*. You're stretching it a bit . . . as usual, Richard."

He was about to offer a retort when the uneasy silence was broken.

"Hello!"

Piruzzi appeared from the side of the house.

"How are you coming along?"

"We were just discussing the design of the garden," I said. "Maybe you can fill us in on its history."

"Ah, yes," said Piruzzi. "But I can only tell you what my grandfather told me. He related the story of how Braegno, my ancestor, built it for his mistresses."

I noticed Clissac shaking her head at Richard. Richard rocked uneasily in his worn-out shoes.

"Women from the village," Piruzzi continued. "The most beautiful virgins, I'm told. They were taken and forced to live here, each in her own house, until Braegno wished to see them. At night, it was said that young men from the village would climb the mountain to see the beauties who had been taken from them by a man from Rome, a man of the church. There are even stories that when Braegno tired of one, she would be thrown from her balcony, only to fall back to the village in death. If you listen you'll hear the birds singing—singing sad songs for those virgins."

He smiled ever so slightly.

"Renzo," said Clissac. "Why the number seven? Why seven pavilions?"

Piruzzi's smile widened and he shrugged.

"Braegno was a busy man with his women, I suppose," he said.

The silence was broken by laughter, softly at first, but then in a roar that even Battle appreciated.

"Now," said the *dottore*. "I suggest that all of you get some rest. We'll dine this evening at eight and begin work in the morning. I am sure that you must be tired from your journey."

The group dispersed. A few of them wandered through the garden pointing out details to one another. Others meandered towards their quarters, disappearing one by one into the pavilions.

"Are you comfortable, Jamie?" Piruzzi asked, once the others had gone.

"I'm fine, Renzo."

Piruzzi wandered over to a stone bench, his gait tentative. He sat down hard, dropping to the marble with more force than I'm sure he had intended. For the first time, he appeared very old to me, and I wondered if he had been made over by a surgeon's knife to appear more youthful. His eyes wandered off to the mountains, and he began to hum an unrecognizable tune.

"Is there anything you want from me?" I asked him. I was hoping that he would fill me in on a few of the competition details. He had been keeping me in the dark, purposefully I had assumed. Maybe now, as we were about to begin, he would bring me up to date.

"No," he answered calmly. His eyes shifted slowly from the distance back to me, and as they refocused, they seemed to reveal that secrecy was still his intention. I looked closely at his face, which though old, and full in every dimension, was noble, with powerful lines that formed sinuous shadows.

"Do you believe the story you told us of your ancestor?" I asked.

His stiff right hand rose and stroked his moustache while he rested the other arm upon his thigh.

"I suppose not," he replied, his intriguing pupils looking straight into mine. "I would hope that he had higher motivation. But the virgin story comforts me in the light of my own vices."

"And what are your vices, if you don't mind my asking?"

"My vices? Not women. I'm too old for that." His face eased into a smile. "I don't know. Power, I suppose. A desire for absolute power is my vice."

"But surely a man in your position—" I said.

"Should have power," he interrupted. *Should*—yes. Oh, I have my empire. I have my company and its employees. I have this villa and several others. I have all the money I could ever want. But that's a power which is contracted. Money enters in. I guess I would like the power a mother has over her child. Power as respect."

I looked at him in silence, unable to respond. As his final words trailed off, he rose unexpectedly and stepped away. He was thinking about something serious, a belief perhaps that his desire for power was consuming him. He walked slowly over the gray granite cobbles of the courtyard. At the entrance to the house, he turned, and in the shadows, nodded to me as if to say, You do understand me, don't you, Ramsgill? I'd have to admit that I didn't.

"Jamie, come have a drink. Dinner's not for ten minutes."

I had just passed Richard Battle's pavilion and was about to enter the dining room of the main house. The sun was just setting, the way it does late on a summer day, and I didn't need to look at my watch to know that I was early for dinner. I had hoped to see Piruzzi.

Battle was standing in his doorway, drink in hand, his dark bony frame backlit by the warm light of his foyer.

His quarters were smaller than mine, with a bedroom on the ground floor and a living room above. We made our way up a narrow staircase and entered the living area, which had been converted into a weekend studio. The furniture had been pushed into a corner and most of the space taken up by a large flat drawing table. On it were the tools of the architect: a parallel edge, triangles, scales, pens, pencils, markers, compasses and the like. Adjacent to the drawing table was a small desk outfitted with pads of paper, reference books (in English), a calculator, an electric typewriter. Next to the desk was another small wooden table, this one covered with model-making materials.

"I'm afraid all I have is scotch—but it's damn good scotch," he said.

"With a little water, please."

He ambled over to his kitchenette to get me a glass.

While waiting I thumbed through some reading material that lay in a haphazard pile on the desk. *Invisible Cities* by Italo Calvino, a book of Adolph Loos essays and the latest issue of the journal *October*.

"Cavalliere and I are going to do just fine together," he said returning to an open whiskey bottle on the desk. "Bunnahabhain. Single malt. You can't get this nectar in the States, you know."

I didn't know. I watched as he poured me a stiff one and noticed that the bottle was already three-quarters gone.

"Better go easy on that," I said when he had finished pouring.

"Jamie, *mio amico*. Why? I'm fully stocked."

He opened a cabinet and showed me several more bottles in his supply.

"Richard . . . it's none of my business . . . but I can't help it. I like you, and though you don't want to hear it from me, you should go easy on the booze. This is a superb opportunity for you. To get your practice back on track."

He stared across at me with eyes full of contempt. He brought me the glass, but rather than handing it to me, he popped it down on the table.

"You're right," he said, laughing a condescending laugh. "I *don't* want to hear it from you. What the fuck do you know about my practice? You're an academic. You've been looking at too much fucking ivy."

I took a deep breath and considered his words. His antagonism was a recent phenomenon, as if the words were coming from someone I no longer knew. What was the point of trying to reason with him anyway? In his state I doubt that my counseling had any meaning.

I tried one more time: "Richard, listen. You've got a one-in-six chance of winning the most important commission of your life."

Something seemed to click. He heard what I was saying. His head dropped a little and he slipped into a wicker chair across the room. He crossed his bony legs, showing a pale white calf above his red socks.

"I'm not going to win," he said. He spoke softly, like a child admitting a lie.

"Come on," I said. "You've got as good a chance as anybody."

I waited for a reaction, but I got none.

"Look at the competition," I continued against his silence. "First of all, you've got Garbutt and Keller. They're too old to compete. I doubt that either of them has been at a drawing table in decades. Hara, well, he's good, but my intuition tells me that his work is not the kind of thing Piruzzi would go for. Clissac, maybe, but she's awfully theoretical. Her work's not exactly easy to take for a non-architect. And Borromini, I doubt it. His ideas are too extreme."

Battle's bloodshot eyes wandered across the ceiling slowly before settling into his cupped hands. They were sunken eyes, eyes full of pain.

"Not to disagree with you," he said. "I like the idea of winning. But for starters, Keller has an added incentive to win."

"And what's that?" I asked.

"You haven't heard? He's filed for bankruptcy."

Keller certainly had his troubles of late, that I knew for sure. And being a person of his stature, they had been reported mercilessly in the press. To begin with, he had just lost a legal suit to a large municipality for structural defects in one of his buildings. Also—and I had just read this in *The New York Times*—his partner of thirty-five years was leaving him. Rumor had it that the partner received an enormous cash settlement. But I thought Keller had deep pockets. I'd heard nothing of bankruptcy.

"Yeah," Richard continued. "When old Bullock walked out of Keller's office he took several million. And most of Keller's clients, too. So Keller must want the competition pretty bad."

"But Keller doesn't have half your talent, Richard. If you ask me, I think it's between Clissac and you—if you don't waste the opportunity, that is."

He caught me eyeing his drink.

"I don't know . . . ," he said, cradling his glass.

"Listen, Richard. I pushed for you to be included in the competition because I believe in your work. When you're on your mark, nobody's better. I told Piruzzi that."

"Seriously?" he said, looking up. "Not just trying to flatter a has-been?"

"We've had this discussion before. You're the only one that thinks you're a has-been."

He sighed.

"You've got to have the right connections now'days, Jamie. It doesn't matter how talented you are. It's who you know."

"And who the hell *don't* you know, Richard? Talk about connections! For Christ's sake, you're a white male who went to Choate. And Yale. You were in Skull and Bones. Your ex-wife is a du Pont."

He smiled a bit. He realized, I think, that connections were not his problem.

"I just can't seem to get the work done anymore," he said. "There's no spark."

"And whose fault is that?" I asked.

"I've lost interest, Jamie. Architecture's become nothing but style. No substance."

"Says who?"

"Look at the ones that've sold out."

Here we go again, I thought. What was his problem? It was as if the mediocre architects of the world were somehow conspiring against him, dragging him down. In fact, it was as if the entire world were dragging him down, and that he had no responsibility for his own predicament.

"But *you* haven't sold out," I said.

"It doesn't matter. People don't want to pay for quality anymore." He stared down at the floor.

"You ever read John Ruskin?" I asked.

"Of course."

"He said the same things you're saying a hundred years ago. Thought the nineteenth century was the end of civilization as we know it. In hindsight it was rather romantic, don't you think?"

He rose and poured himself another scotch. The glass went to his mouth like a magnet to metal. He licked his thin pale lips, then spoke.

"That's bullshit, Jamie. No comparison. The nineteenth century didn't have media hype, for one thing. Journal upon journal of nothing but paper architecture. Paper walls. Architecture made of words, not bricks."

"You actually pay attention to the media?" I asked. "I thought only students read journals. Besides, my livelihood is paper architecture. Those who can't do, teach . . . remember?"

He chuckled reluctantly. It was his first sign of life since I'd joined him.

"Oh fuck, Jamie. I'm not knocking teaching . . . or writing. It's just that most of the profession doesn't give a shit about the craft of building. About seeing a project through. The Thornburgh Kellers of the world are the ones who succeed. He'll find a way to win this thing, even though it's supposed to be fair."

I sighed. His pessimism was contagious. "It'll be fair, Richard. Give it a chance, huh? You've got a lot left in you."

"Do I? Seems I'm constantly running into walls."

I rose and set down my drink. Through Battle's front window I could see activity in the dining room.

"Brick walls, or paper?"

I turned, just as a smile emerged from his twisted face. I knew that I had him. For the moment anyway, he had relented.

THREE

The moment didn't last too long, because less than eight hours later Richard Battle was dead. I was asleep in my pavilion when I was awakened, first by the rumble of distant thunder, and then by a knock at my door. I checked my watch. It was five fifteen A.M. Over at the front window, I rubbed what little sleep I had managed to get from my eyes. I could see that the cobblestones were wet with dew, light reflecting from the tops of those closest to the house. Below me Cavalliere stood at my door. At the other end of the garden I could see Piruzzi, nervously pacing just outside the open doorway to Richard's pavilion.

I dressed quickly. I then stumbled downstairs and opened the door.

"Come quick," said Cavalliere.

We hurried across the garden, my mind lodged on the thought that something terrible had happened. We reached the pavilion and approached Piruzzi. The look on his face confirmed my fears of the worst.

"Your friend," Piruzzi said. "He's dead."

My first thought was of Richard's daughter of seventeen. Like her father she was emotional, with the added frailty of adolescence. I would have to be the one to tell her.

"How?" I said, almost in a whisper. "What happened?"

"We don't know for sure," said Piruzzi. "We think he choked."

"Where is he?" I asked.

"Upstairs. You can see him, but don't disturb things. I must call the police."

Piruzzi excused himself, and Cavalliere and I climbed the stairs. We were met by the odor of alcohol, and something sour, like urine.

Richard was sitting in the same wicker chair as when I had joined him prior to dinner, his mouth open, a blank stare directed up towards the ceiling. He was wearing light blue silk pajamas, and his hair was mussed. The pain was gone from his eyes, and ironically, he looked more peaceful now than he had in years, as if the weight of the whole world had floated away from him, which is, in a way, what had happened.

I had never seen a dead body before, at least not in an unembalmed state. His skin had a pale brown tint to it, an opacity marked by a retreat of the tiny pink capillaries that normally color white flesh. The only place this differed was around his eyes, where the blood vessels stood out unnaturally. His forehead held the remnants of sweat beads. Below his mouth the flecked ringlets of facial hair that made up his beard were stained, and there beneath his long angular neck, more of the stain, deep red atop the shoulders of his pajama shirt. The stains stopped abruptly at his chest though, and the whole gave the appearance of crimson epaulets. From the rear, more of the stain covered his back. His shoulders slumped with an odd ease, and his hands rested in his lap. His brittle fingers were entwined in a forceful embrace.

"A terrible situation," said Cavalliere.

"Who found him?" I asked weakly. I slumped into a nearby chair.

"I did," Cavalliere said. "I awoke and from my room in the house I could see down into his studio. I saw him through the window sitting in this chair. I knew how much he had been drinking and thought I would come help him to bed. When I got here, he was like this."

"What'd you do then?"

"I woke the *dottore.*"

"And you came back here?"

"Yes."

"Did anyone call a doctor?"

"There was no need to. He was clearly dead. The *dottore* said he would contact the authorities."

I returned my gaze to Richard and thought of his condition when I had seen him last.

We had dined at eight in the great hall, a room the size of a two-story house. Piruzzi prepared a gracious table—*trota con salsa pecieda, crespelle ai quattro formaggi, insalata del mar.* The food was accompanied by innumerable bottles of the local Valpolicella Classico, and none of us was feeling any pain. Richard was clearly drunk, belligerent and morose, but surprisingly he was kept up with by the others, particularly Sir Colin, who matched him glass for glass.

Around ten we adjourned to the library for dessert and espresso, where we stayed until retiring for the night. When jet lag and Richard's ravings had finally gotten the better of me, I retired, leaving several of the others behind.

"What time did he leave the library last night?" I asked Cavalliere, still staring at Richard's lifeless frame.

"I don't know, sir. The *dottore* dismissed me at midnight. Mr. Battle was still in the library."

"Was he alone?"

"No sir. He was with the English gentleman. And Borromini, I believe."

I walked to the window and stared across the black garden. Garbutt's pavilion showed no sign of life. He or Borromini were the last to see Richard alive. I returned to Richard's body thinking about wine.

The stains I had first noticed on his beard and pajama

shirt I now realized must be wine. The bottle next to him on the table was not scotch, but rather it was a bottle of Recioto, the regional dessert wine we had drunk after dinner. It was almost empty and next to it was a half-full claret glass. I leaned over and sniffed from the glass. It was wine all right—ruby red, tannic, concentrated, with a hint of spice, or chestnuts, perhaps.

Next to the glass was a loaf of bread. It was a simple long loaf, broken in the middle, a few crumbs scattered about the surface of the table. It seemed an odd choice for a midnight snack.

"Those stains are unusual, don't you think?"

"Are they, sir?"

"His shoulders are saturated and his back is covered, but the front of his shirt's clean. It's as though he were drinking lying down."

Cavalliere didn't answer.

"And what's the bread for?" I wondered aloud.

He shrugged.

I hung around a bit more, careful not to disturb things, before realizing that there was nothing else I could do. I was anguished by what had taken place, and mad. Mad at Richard for not taking better care of himself, mad at myself for not stepping in to help.

I left the studio and walked back downstairs. I stood at the door of the pavilion, breathing in the damp pre-dawn air. I then crossed the courtyard and rapped lightly at Sir Colin's door. There was no answer, so I tried again. This time the door was pulled back, and Sir Colin stood before me tying the sash to his burgundy bathrobe.

"Yes? What is it?"

"Sir Colin," I said. "A terrible thing has happened. Richard's dead."

His old eyes widened.

"How perfectly dreadful, Ramsgill. What happened?"

"Perhaps he choked. Or drank too much. He was found by Cavalliere up in his studio."

"What time is it?" he asked.

I stared down at my wrist. The luminous dials to my sport watch stood out against the dark. "Almost five thirty," I said.

"Well he was certainly paralytic when we set off for bed," Sir Colin said.

"What?"

"Drunk out of his mind. I thought that he and Borromini were going to come to blows. Polemic arguments, that type of thing. Battle against the world, especially against what Borromini stood for."

I paused and reflected upon what he said. I then recalled how it had all started, just after dinner, when Borromini, Keller and I had walked into the library together.

"I tell you gentlemen," Borromini had said as we entered the library. He had joined us from Rome just before dinner. "Piruzzi has no idea—not a clue—of what he has here."

He was referring to the villa, and especially the space we were in. It was a warm paneled room that might have been mistaken for an art gallery. Veronese hung alongside De Chirico, Mantegna next to Paladino, all in the company of fine rugs and antiques.

Borromini grabbed my forearm.

"Look at that, would you? The complexity of that cornice, the way it writhes along the edge of the frescoes. My God in heaven!"

He was pointing to the ceiling, which was a complex composition of gilded plaster moldings inset with murals on some religious theme. His passion for what lay overhead was not lost on me. Of the competition architects, his affinity for the past was the strongest and best known. In a world of modern architects, Borromini was an avowed traditionalist.

He scorned modern architecture. In fact, he rejected all forms of contemporary creature comfort, no matter how radical his position. Recently, for example, he had espoused abolition of the automobile as a cure for the urban ills of our time. I had read an article he had written in *Casabella,* arguing that cars were simultaneously destroying the environment and a culture based on interactive socialization. He wanted to return to a simpler past, a past based on humanism, a culture infused with a *sensus communis.* The few projects he had managed to complete were based on these ideals. They were built by hand—his stone chiseled by hammer, his beams hewn by axe, his carpet woven on pedal-powered looms. And above all, they were based on Italian classicism, where he believed humanism to lie.

To look at him, you'd never know that he had such ideals. He was a good-looking man in his early fifties, with straight jet black hair and a classic jaw. His dress was the epitome of Italian high style—a black linen shirt with mother-of-pearl and sterling silver buttons, baggy cotton trousers of exaggerated houndstooth, designer tortoise-shell eyeglasses. As he studied the murals over our heads, I couldn't help thinking that he looked like a Georges Marciano model.

"Stealing ideas?"

Richard Battle walked in behind us. His lower lip protruded the way it always did when he had had too much to drink.

"I'm sorry?" said Borromini.

"Just caught you ogling. Since you have no original ideas of your own, you must be cribbing some for the competition."

Richard's words came with a slow deliberateness, but he slurred them just the same. By now Piruzzi had also joined us.

Borromini smiled. "Richard," he said, "you never change."

"You two know each other?" I asked.

"We've debated a few times. The Stockholm conference, two years ago. Right, Richard?"

Richard's mouth warmed into a perverse smile. "Yep," he said. "And your work, Gio, it's definitely retrogressed since then. I've been keeping up with you."

"Battle," Keller said. "Lighten up."

"It's quite all right, Thornburgh. I'll take it as a compliment. Retrogression, that is. Maybe you would do well to apply historical methods, Richard."

"Right," I said. "And you can expect Madonna to join a nunnery." If there was one thing you could say about Richard's work, it was that it was highly original and never derivative.

"I've learned from history," Battle responded. "And it teaches the architect to be of his own time. Name your architect. Callicrates? Suger? Michelangelo? They each built for their own time, and *of* their own time. What makes you think classicism has any relevance in the today's world?"

"It has the same cultural relevance," Borromini said, "that religion and philosophy have."

"Religion, shit! You Catholics are a pious lot. I'll grant you that philosophy has a place. But classicism and religion are as dead as Caesar's ghost."

"Afraid not, my friend," Borromini said. "Italian classicism, the mother of architecture, is timeless. It's as good for the modern world as it was for the ancients."

Piruzzi smiled and fingered his moustache.

"Oh, Italian it has to be, huh?" Battle said.

Borromini nodded.

"We're not forgetting the minor contribution of the Greeks, are we?" Battle continued. "As in the invention of the classical style?"

"If I may interrupt," Piruzzi said, "Gio tells me that what the Greeks did was sculpture, not architecture."

I looked to Borromini for an explanation.

"It's true," he said shrugging. "With the Greeks, everything was the temple. But the temple isn't architecture as we know it. It's one room, or at most, two. It took the Romans to invent the forum, the stadium, the basilica, the baths, the great cities and so on. Not to mention the contribution of Italy later on—in the Renaissance, that is."

Cavalliere approached us with a tray of drinks. Battle deposited his empty, and we took glasses from the tray. Cavalliere hesitated in order to gauge our reaction. It was a powerful dessert wine, dry and velvety with a hint of cherries.

"Very good," Keller said. "What is it? Chianti?"

Borromini laughed. "To you Americans," he said, "all Italian wine is Chianti."

"It's the best of our local wines . . . Recioto Amarone," answered Piruzzi. "The wine maker, Bertani, is a friend of mine."

"And I suppose that the Italians make the best wine in the world, too," said Battle, finishing his glass. He immediately took a second drink and looked towards Piruzzi with glazed eyes.

"But of course," answered Borromini.

"Sounds like you two have it all figured out," I said. "Renzo, if you feel so strongly about Italian architecture, then why'd you invite the others to compete? You should just have Borromini do your building."

There was a brief silence, followed by a spurt of laughter.

"Borromini speaks for himself," Piruzzi chuckled. "While I obviously love my native architecture, I have no preconceptions, as I told you in my letters. I want the most brilliant design, whatever that might be."

"Zeitgeist," said Battle.

"Classical refinement," chided Borromini.

"I still don't get it," persisted Battle, slurping his drink. "I mean . . . how does Gio enjoy the reputation he does when he's simply regurgitating the past? It's ludicrous."

"The past," Borromini said coolly, "is understandable to the common man."

"The hell with the common man, you fucking Luddite!" snapped Battle. The others in the room turned towards our group. The discussion was deteriorating.

"Let's save our energy for the competition," I said.

"Per favore," Piruzzi echoed.

Borromini then excused himself and joined the others across the room. I put my hand on Richard's shoulder.

"I'm tired," I said. "How about you? Ready for bed?"

He shook his head like a pouting child.

"You need some sleep, Richard."

"Fuck off," he said, and he wandered towards the bar.

I shrugged, offering apologies to Piruzzi before saying good night. I assumed that Richard and Borromini had ended their tiff. However, it seemed from what Sir Colin was now telling me that they hadn't. And now, just a few hours later, Richard was dead.

"What time did you leave the library?" I asked Sir Colin.

"The others left about midnight. Battle and I stayed until well after one. He kept up his verbal assault against Borromini, the others, his ex-wife. Finally, I was knackered and told him I was heading off. Had to coax him along, really. Saw him to his door."

"Was Borromini with you?"

"No. He left earlier."

Just then the sound of a car came from the front of the house.

"Did Richard take anything to drink along with him to his pavilion?" I asked.

Sir Colin craned his neck in the direction of the noise. He then returned his gaze to me and thought for a moment.

"He had a bottle of wine," he said.

"Yes?"

"Uh-huh. After the others had gone, there was an extra bottle of that dessert wine we were drinking. He dipped into it."

"The Recioto?" I asked.

"That's right."

"Was it a full bottle?"

"Well, it was. But by the time we left, he had finished it."

"But I thought you said he took it along with him to his pavilion."

"He did—the bottle, that is. But it was empty."

"Then why'd he take it along?"

"I don't know. Let me think. As I said, he was soused. Yes . . . he had been drinking directly from the bottle in the library. When he finished it, I suggested we retire. He could hardly speak at this point. I figured he was going to have a whale of a hangover, not exactly the way to begin Piruzzi's competition. He was just sitting on the couch in front of the fireplace, cradling the bottle and mumbling about how his wife had ruined his career by leaving him. I really felt sorry for the chap. Anyway, I managed to get him to come along with me, but he wouldn't relinquish that bottle. He was clutching it like a child's teddy. I saw no harm in it, so I saw him to his door, and that was that. And now he's dead. How strange the way these things happen."

"How drunk would you say he was?"

"Very."

"Could he have simply overdosed on alcohol? Or was he so drunk that he could have choked on the wine?"

"He drank an extraordinary amount. I'm a tippling man myself, but I was no match for him. He was well off the deep end, that's for sure."

I heard a door opening somewhere up near the main house. A moment later Piruzzi and two men hurried across the garden and into Battle's pavilion.

"That must be the police," I said. "By the way, did he have a loaf of bread with him when you walked him back to the pavilion?"

"A loaf of bread?" answered Garbutt. "What on earth for?"

"I don't know. But one was found next to him. On a table with the wine."

"How odd. How very odd."

* * *

A handsome middle-aged man wearing a gabardine trenchcoat was drawing blood from Richard's forearm as I again entered the studio. He looked more like an actor than a medical examiner, but he must have been the latter, because an open satchel of instruments rested on the floor next to his kneeling form. He had a narrow face with bronze skin, long dark hair which he parted in the middle, and ardent eyes, the kind made for the big screen. He seemed indifferent to the dead man before him, and instead was preoccupied with the surroundings.

"Very nice, your villa," he said to Piruzzi, who along with Cavalliere stood beside him. "I like that painting."

My eyes followed his to the far wall of the studio, where above the travertine fireplace an oil painting of a full-figured nude woman hung in an elaborate, gilt frame. She was bathing with some swans and painted with mottled pink skin, emblematic of a lesser baroque artist—at least to my eyes the work seemed to be baroque.

"Ari, stop daydreaming and move over! I'm trying to take a picture here!"

The voice came from my left, where from behind a philodendron, a balding man in black glasses stood. In his left hand was a dusty old box camera and in his right, extended above his head, an aluminum reflector with a built-in flashbulb unit, the kind I hadn't seen since Fellini's *La Dolce Vita*.

The doctor shuffled out of the other man's way, then removed the needle from Richard's arm. The balding man snapped a picture.

"Ah, Ramsgill," Piruzzi said.

"Who are you?" asked the balding man as he turned towards me. He had a gravelly voice, and the tone of the question seemed less like a true display of interest than an indictment of my presence before him.

"James Ramsgill," I answered. "I'm an advisor to Dottor Piruzzi . . . on his competition."

"What competition?"

"I've invited six architects," said Piruzzi to the man in rapid Italian, "to compete this weekend for the commission to design our new world headquarters."

"I see," said the bald man.

Piruzzi then turned to me.

"Professor Ramsgill," he said. "This is Inspector Constaga Anghini. And Dr. Stavalos, the medical examiner, from Brescia."

Dr. Stavalos nodded, still working at Richard's side. Anghini offered me a limp hand. As he shook he fished a crumpled pack of cigarettes from the pocket of his leather jacket and searched the other parts of his clothing for a match.

"Professor Ramsgill was a friend of Mr. Battle's," said Piruzzi.

Anghini withdrew his hand and lit his cigarette.

"Then I would like to ask you a few questions." He exhaled some smoke in my direction.

He had thin black hair and not much of it, but what he did have had been combed carefully and held in place by oil. There was very little hair on the top of his head, and a few select strands barely concealed the bumpy liver-spotted surface of his flat skull. His bifocals were large, and they seemed embedded into a hook nose, the nose in turn hanging down over a sculpted moustache and a thin mouth.

"The *dottore* tells me Mr. Battle was very drunk tonight," he continued, speaking through dark brown lips. He had a small gap between his top two incisors, and as he talked his cigarette bounced like an errant surfboard coming off a pounding wave.

I considered the statement, which upon reflection was in need of clarification.

"Richard had a problem with alcohol," I said.

"Was he prone to drinking himself unconscious?"

"I don't really know," I answered. "While we were professional friends, we didn't socialize much. There have been times when I've seen him drunk . . . but never passed out."

Anghini gazed down at his rough hands.

"So he might have drunk himself to death?" he asked. He began to pick at a cuticle, and I noticed the dark stains that longtime smokers have at their fingertips.

"I suppose so . . . except for what Sir Colin said."

"Who's Sir Colin?"

"Sir Colin Garbutt," answered Piruzzi. "Another of my architects. Apparently he was the last one to see Mr. Battle alive."

"And what did this Sir Colin have to say?"

"I've just spoken with him," I said. "Richard was drunk all right, that we all knew. The funny thing is, though, Sir Colin says that he came to the pavilion with an *empty* bottle of wine."

"But there's wine in the bottle . . . and in the glass," said Piruzzi.

"Sir Colin said it was empty."

"Maybe your Englishman's wrong," said Anghini. "Or maybe Mr. Battle had another bottle here in the pavilion."

"No," I said. "If he'd wanted something else to drink, he would have drunk scotch. He'd already begun hoarding for the weekend."

I walked over to the cabinet in which Richard kept his scotch and opened it. The nearly empty bottle from the previous afternoon was there, along with three others.

"See."

"He's right, sir," said Cavalliere. "I brought Mr. Battle four full bottles of scotch this afternoon."

Anghini then paused for a moment before saying: "Did Mr. Battle have a history of health problems? Other than this drinking problem?"

"Not that I know of," I said. "He had a bad back, like most architects."

"Was he taking any medications?"

"I don't know."

"Anything else I should know about?"

"Nothing I can think of."

"Was he depressed?"

I considered the implication of the question. That Richard had committed suicide.

"Sort of," I said.

"Constaga, come here."

Dr. Stavalos drew our attention towards Richard's body. He had a small flashlight out and he was looking into Richard's mouth.

"I think we can forget about too much alcohol," he said. "Or suicide, for that matter. Look here, there's something lodged in his throat. It's the bread, I suspect."

We moved closer.

"Notice the redness around his cheekbones," Dr. Stavalos continued. "And under the eyes. That's pete-chial hemorrhaging."

"What?" I said.

"Petechial hemorrhaging," said Stavalos. "A sign of asphyxiation."

"He choked on the bread?" Piruzzi asked.

"So it would appear," said Stavalos. "He may have been drunk, but short of an autopsy I'd say the cause of death was asphyxiation by an obstructed trachea. Not surprising, given the fact that he was inebriated."

Anghini waved us off as if we were beggar children. He then took six or eight close-up photographs of Richard's mouth and head, each time shifting his view slightly in order to fully realize the body's position in the chair. When he was finished, he stepped away until he was a good ten feet from the body. He snapped one last photo.

Stavalos started depositing instruments into his bag, then he slowly buckled it, and rose.

"Are you ready, Inspector?"

Anghini was fumbling to get the spent flash attachment off of his camera.

"Yes," he said.

"The hospital crew's on its way for the body," Dr.

Stavalos said to Piruzzi. "I'm officially pronouncing him dead, which is my only responsibility at this unusual hour."

He and Anghini started slowly towards the stairs. As they were about to descend, Anghini turned back, his inquiring eyes moving to Richard's body.

"One more question, Professor Ramsgill," he said. "Did your friend get along with the other architects that are competing for Dottor Piruzzi's commission?"

The question caught me by surprise. I turned to Richard and considered his irascibility, considered what his drinking had done to his career, where his personality had left him in life, and now death.

"Unfortunately," I said a moment later, "Richard didn't get along with anyone. Not even himself."

FOUR

A fitful lizard clung to the worn white balustrade, its compact blue shadow hugging the cool stone. It ran a few steps, hesitated, jerked its head from side to side, then froze again. After a few seconds of absolute stillness, I watched it dart off, this time disappearing over the side of the balustrade and into the brush.

We were gathered for breakfast on the outdoor dining terrace, the coolness of the morning doing nothing to quell the sorrow I felt within. The solemnity on each architect's face was clearly evident, though I suspected less out of real grief for Richard Battle than for fear that the competition would now be canceled. Piruzzi looked genuinely despondent, as if Richard's death had sucked something of life right out of him. His eyes were vacuous, he ate slowly, and he seemed a different person from the one whose shrewdness had earlier impressed me.

"We all now know of our friend's death," he said as the meal wound down.

"It was from too much alcohol?" Gio Borromini asked from my left.

"Probably not," Piruzzi said. "According to Dr. Stavalos, wine is not potent enough to have killed him. He thinks he choked to death on a piece of bread."

"A piece of bread?" asked Pet Clissac. She was just spreading jam onto a bit of toast. She stopped spreading and placed the toast back on her plate.

"Yes," said Piruzzi. "A loaf was on the table next to him. He was extremely drunk, and he must have succumbed when a bit of the bread went down the wrong tube."

"C'est dommage," Pet muttered. She stared down at the toast, pondering whether to eat it.

"Frankly I'm not sure of the next step," said Piruzzi. "The authorities tell me that it may be several days, if not longer, before Mr. Battle's body will be returned to America. I suppose we should think about canceling the competition under the circumstances, or at least delaying it by a few days until we get our spirits up again. I'm thinking particularly of Professor Ramsgill."

The group was silent before Akio Hara spoke.

"It would be wise to delay the competition," he said. "Out of respect. We could rearrange our schedules to accommodate this."

Thornburgh Keller pushed himself back from the table. He raised an eyebrow and dabbed the corner of his turned-down mouth with a napkin.

"Speak for yourself," he said. "I have to be in Berlin on Tuesday and Toronto the day after. My calendar is booked months in advance. I can't delay my work here. Not a single hour."

Piruzzi weighed the statement before speaking again.

"What do the others of you think?" he asked.

"I'm with Hara," said Sir Colin. "I can wait, if it's your wish."

He nodded slowly as he looked around the table, seeming to solicit support.

"That's because you're not overwhelmed with work," Pet Clissac snapped. "I don't have the luxury of time. We didn't come here for a holiday, Garbutt. I'm with Keller. We should go on."

"And you, Gio?" said Piruzzi.

The Italian Borromini sat up and ran his fingers back through his hair. His hair was full of body, and it fell back to its exact former location. He was unshaven, with a heavy shadow covering the lower part of his face.

"I vote to go on," he said, looking at me. "Waiting will do no good. No disrespect to Richard, but I believe he would feel the same way, given the circumstances."

"That leaves you, Professor Ramsgill."

I considered Borromini's statement. I wondered if Richard would have voted to go on. I then thought of my own situation, in light of what the others had said. Of all the people around the table, I probably had the most time on my hands. I didn't have an office to rush back to, no employees beckoning for instruction. My plans after the competition were unsettled. The fall semester wouldn't start for another month, and my planned jaunt around the Continent was certainly not urgent. My grief for Richard was real, but I wasn't sure that delaying things would help.

"It doesn't matter," I said. "I can stay longer. But if Thornburgh and Pet can't afford the time, I wouldn't oppose going on, either."

Piruzzi looked to Hara and Garbutt, who were the only ones to propose postponement. They nodded their approval to begin again.

Piruzzi then stood.

"I must admit I hadn't expected this," he said as his eyes swept around the table.

"If this is the wish, though, then we shall begin as if nothing ever happened. Once we start, however, no one can change his mind. I shall treat the competition just as I had originally planned. If you change your mind, you're out."

My colleagues didn't protest.

"Then we shall discuss my program for the competition and the rules under which you shall work. Franco?"

Cavalliere began handing out packets prepared for the competitors. The thin packets were bound in a yellow folder that each architect began to study as he or she received it.

"Also, I hope that this program doesn't change anyone's mind," said Piruzzi.

I read the title page of the packet I was handed: PROGRAM FOR DESIGN OF A CHAPEL ON THE GROUNDS OF THE VILLA PIRUZZI, SALÒ, ITALY. I thumbed through it quickly.

"This isn't a corporate headquarters," said Thornburgh Keller. "What's going on?"

"Exactly as you read," said Piruzzi. "We'll be designing a chapel. Not an office building."

"What's the meaning of this?" asked Garbutt. "I didn't come all this way to spend time on such a piddling project. I can't do this in my office with the kind of projects we do. I need big work, that pays."

"The fee, my friend, will be no different from that if you were designing my headquarters building."

"But you've duped us," Garbutt said. "If I had known that you wanted a chapel, I would have prepared differently. I don't like this!" His face twitched nervously and was markedly red.

Piruzzi leaned forward, resting the palms of his hands on the table, just beyond his plate.

"Any of you," he said softly, but with a tone of authority, "who wants to bow out this very moment is welcome to. I'll not waste my money on those unwilling to compete. Those who stay will play by my rules. If you win the award, the fee will still be five million dollars."

Silence. It was as if the words "five million" were an opiate and the designers addicts.

"But why a chapel?" I asked, now understanding Piruzzi's reason for not letting me in on the details of the competition. "Why pay several million dollars to an architect for such a small building? The prize money alone is probably in excess of what it will take to build the building."

He shrugged. "Maybe, maybe not. As I told you yesterday, Jamie, I have all the money I will ever need. I'm old. I'll not be around forever. A new headquarters for

Piruzzi S.p.A. I don't need. Something that makes me feel good spiritually, I do."

"But—" Clissac started.

"Let me finish, please," Piruzzi said. "I don't want just a chapel. I want the greatest chapel ever designed. As great as the Sistine or the Medici. With the quality of light that one senses at Chartres. The feeling of space that Le Corbusier captured at Notre Dame du Haut. The movement one feels in Bernini's *Sant'Agnese*. I've gathered the pre-eminent architects of the world, and I have done so not without reason. Money is no object. But I want it to be the best!"

"But why didn't you tell us of your plans earlier?" asked Clissac.

Piruzzi's eyes lit up.

"Ah," he said. "For two reasons. One, if I had told you that the competition was to be for the design of a chapel, many of you, like my friend from England here, might have thought it too small and not come. Second, by surprising you, I'm assured that no one will have worked on the project ahead of time. As Garbutt said, he would have prepared differently. For all I know, each of you may have a design for the Piruzzi headquarters building already formulated in your head, if not on paper."

Quiet around the table. The silence confirmed his allegation.

"So," he continued. "Does anyone want to bow out?"

I knew the answer to that question. Who wouldn't compete, even under the circumstances Piruzzi had defined?

"Then we shall begin. I'll not bore you with a recitation of what's contained in the packet. Read it carefully. It describes the desired spaces and functions for the chapel as well as engineering information about the site, which, by the way, is down below the walls of the villa in the woods. I would, however, like to describe my rules for the game. I have but a few. As you know, you will work alone. And as I believe you have been told, professional questions should be directed to Professor Ramsgill. We'll not work in the evening, at least not around dinner. We'll eat together in the dining hall, retire for dessert, and if you must, as I know you architects think you must, once you return to quarters you are free to work longer. No one leaves the villa grounds during the competition. You'll be allowed no outside correspondence, unless it's an emergency. I have but one way of ensuring that you do the work on your own, and this is it. Anyone caught violating these rules will be disqualified and asked to withdraw. You'll be returned to Verona for the next available flight home. Am I clear?"

A leaden silence hovered over the table. Piruzzi seemed to have recovered from his angst in the face of Richard's death. Watching him was like watching a father admonishing his children, and he seemed to enjoy it. The funny thing is that they all took it. No one raised an objection.

"When do we begin?" Keller finally asked sheepishly, once he was sure that the *dottore* had had his say.

"Right away," Piruzzi answered. "There's no need to wait. I'll leave you to it momentarily and see you for dinner at eight. You'll come to breakfast two days from now with your completed drawings. And, gentlemen and Mme. Clissac, I have one more thing to reveal to you. Franco?"

Piruzzi's eyes wandered across the terrace.

Cavalliere appeared from the door to the dining room carrying a large wooden box. As he brought it closer, I could see that it was made of walnut, deep rich brown with black figuring in the grain of the wood. It was an old box, scarred and worn, and its top was made up to look like a Roman temple. Four half-round ebony columns with capitals of lapis lazuli centered the composition. The columns held up an entablature and a triangular pediment, each constructed of *trompe-l'oeil* marquetry. The marquetry was formed of various woods—cherry, bass, rosewood, and ash—the lighter woods representing part of the form in sunlight, the darker ones representing shadows. The precision of the inlay told my eyes that the box had been constructed by a master wood-carver, and also that the box was meant to hold something of great importance.

Cavalliere carefully set the box on the table. He then placed his heavy thumb on the two-dimensional "steps" of the temple. Sliding them to one side he revealed a brass latching mechanism, which upon being pressed, caused the column front and pediment above to hinge open as if by magic, slowly and without much force, until the contents of this enigmatic box were revealed.

"My God," I said almost in a whisper.

My comment was not directed at the legerdemain involved in opening the box, but rather at what lay inside. Before us was a manuscript in codex form, made up of numerous sheets of paper, loosely bound by a leather cord. The paper was parchment, long since faded and curled, and the writing Latin. It took me a moment to decipher the title.

"It can't be real," said Pet Clissac, looking at the manuscript before us.

"What is it?" asked Thornburgh Keller, an erudite man, but one who obviously did not read Latin.

What it was, or what it certainly appeared to me to be, was a codex version of the Roman Vitruvius Pollio's *De architectura,* or as it is commonly known in English, the *Ten Books on Architecture.* Vitruvius was an architect and engineer who lived in the first century B.C. Translations of his treatise have survived as the oldest and most influential work on architecture in existence. In the *Ten Books* he expounds upon the full range of classical architecture, introducing along the way the principles of architectural symmetry, harmony and proportion, as well as describing the orders and their use in the buildings of ancient Rome.

To my knowledge, though, only medieval translations of Vitruvius existed. Certainly the form of the text before us, made up of a collection of double-wide papers, each folded once vertically and known as a two-leaf quire, replicated numerous times in a stack, was the common method of producing a medieval manuscript. When a copy of *De architectura* was first discovered in 1414 and translated into medieval Latin, that document, once distributed, became the major impetus for the Renaissance, at least as far as architecture was concerned. My imperfect Latin, however, told me that what now lay before us was not medieval Latin, but classical. Yet if it were truly classical—that is, from Vitruvius's own time—then something was amiss. For the form of the manuscript was not that of a *volumen,* or papyrus roll, the predecessor of the quire. And most likely *De architectura* would have been disseminated in roll form. I had heard of quire forms existing from the first century B.C., but generally they would only have been used as an author's first draft of a work.

I looked harder at the document. The paper was indeed parchment, made no doubt from animal skin and considered inferior to papyrus. The writing was in ink. I noticed scribbles in the margins, margins that were otherwise of a uniform width. Also, at the bottom of the first page, there were additional notes. The longer I looked at the document the more unsure I became. Because if what we were looking at was truly from the first century and if it was not a facsimile or a forgery, then the scribbles and notes, along with the fact that the manuscript was in codex form, could only mean one thing. The manuscript was in the hand of the author. Vitruvius. Vitruvius Pollio. And if that was the case, then it was the architectural equivalent of the discovery of the Dead Sea scrolls.

"It's a manuscript copy of Vitruvius," Pet Clissac said, in answer to Keller's question.

Keller's aged eyes lit up. "You mean from the Middle Ages?" he asked.

"Probably," said Pet.

"No," I said. "It's classical."

I turned to Piruzzi, who was fingering his moustache, and who had a look on his face that was beyond description. "Renzo," I said. "It's not just classical, is it?"

"No, Jamie, it's more than that."

I didn't know how to ask the next question. There was the possibility that Piruzzi's answer might change the history of Western architecture.

I took a deep breath and said: "It's in Vitruvius's own hand."

Piruzzi nodded.

"It's his own draft copy. It's a two-thousand-year-old author's draft of the most important work on architecture ever written."

Again he nodded.

"Where the hell did you get it?" I asked.

Piruzzi laughed softly as he watched Keller slowly turn through the pages that had been removed from the box by Cavalliere.

"That I cannot tell you. Let us just say that it has recently been discovered."

"It must be worth a fortune," Keller said.

"Slight understatement," I said. "But its real value is not monetary. It's as an artifact. At least in so far as Renzo will allow access to it."

I again turned toward Piruzzi.

"You'll allow it to be studied, won't you?"

Piruzzi brought his hands up from the table to his waist. He tucked two thumbs into his belt.

"It's not for me to say," he replied with a sly grin.

"What do you mean?"

"After this weekend," he said, "the manuscript won't belong to me."

"What?" said Borromini.

"The winner of the competition," Piruzzi said sedately, "will come to own the manuscript. I'm offering it as an additional prize."

I can hardly describe the collective look upon the faces of the architects surrounding me. In fact, I wish I could have seen my own jaw drop. Keller leaned forward and fingered the manuscript as if he were selecting diamonds. Clissac lit another cigarette and sat back smugly, perhaps with the belief that her talent would secure the manuscript for herself. Hara looked around at each of us, excitement glistening in his eyes, his brilliant teeth frozen into a broad crescent-shaped grin. Even Garbutt, who earlier had protested Piruzzi's program, was shaking his head as a distinct sign of approval and laughing like a schoolboy.

"Do you mean," said Hara, "that the winner will take both the commission *and* the manuscript?"

"Exactly."

"You can't do that," Borromini protested. His was the only face that displayed a serious expression.

"What do you mean?" said Thornburgh Keller, now thumbing through the manuscript's pages. "Of course he can. He can do anything he damn well pleases."

Borromini reached out and clamped down hard on Keller's wrist.

"You son of a bitch!" Keller cried. He shrank back in pain.

"Gentlemen!" Piruzzi cried.

Keller glowered at Borromini. After a moment Borromini let go of his arm.

"This text belongs to Rome," Borromini said angrily, turning to Piruzzi. "It belongs to Italia. You can't just give it away. What do you mean, *Dottore?*"

"I mean," said Piruzzi as he took the stack of papers from Keller, "that the manuscript goes to the winner of my competition. As I've stated, I want the greatest chapel the world has ever seen to be designed by one of you. That's all. And if Vitruvius will aid in that endeavor, then so be it."

Borromini's eyes hurtled around the table and his jaw tightened.

"Then I shall resign from the competition!" he snapped, pushing his chair back in a rage. He sprang up and rapped his knuckles sharply on the table.

"Do as you like," Piruzzi said coolly. "But by doing so you will only be ensuring that the Vitruvius will leave the country. The only way you can keep it here is to win the competition. Am I right?"

Borromini's face was markedly flush. He didn't speak. He worked his normally animated lips into a frozen line before turning and stomping away.

There was a stunned silence around the table.

"Sorry," Piruzzi finally said after Borromini had disappeared into the garden. "But I'm sure Gio will come around. As for the rest of you . . . am I to assume that you understand everything? And that you are prepared to start work?"

No one spoke up. That was the spell the Vitruvian manuscript had cast.

Then, slowly, one by one, the architects rose and each left the house for the pavilions.

"I guess you know now why I didn't let you in on more details earlier," Piruzzi said to me after everyone else had gone.

I nodded.

"Sorry to do that to you. But this Vitruvius manuscript . . . I had to be absolutely sure that no one knew."

"I understand."

"Fine. Now, do you have all the information you need to do your job?"

I glanced down at the chapel program, which I had rolled up in my left hand.

"I'll give it a quick read," I said. "It seems straightforward."

"Don't hesitate to contact me," he said. "I want to be kept up-to-date on how the competition is going. I believe you should try to see the competitors a few times each day to gauge their progress. I would also like you to keep a written record of your observations."

"Sure," I said.

"And don't feel that you have to adhere to the rules for

the competition. You're free to roam when not keeping an eye on our architects."

I had no desire to go anywhere. And since I had to be available for questions anyway, I intended to stay in my quarters, reading or working on course outlines. I also hoped Piruzzi would let me spend some time looking at the manuscript.

"I'll be around," I said.

"Good. And one more thing, Jamie. I don't want you to think that because I'm paying no attention to the matter, I have forgotten your friend Battle. However, if the competition is to be a success, then we must put this behind us."

I agreed.

The villa was just waking to the eastern sun, now well over the lake. In the far distance tiny boats crept like insects across the vast blue water, while nearer, the faint whine of trucks rose from the road that skirted the shore. There was a placid calm in the garden, as if the villa had been separated from the rest of humanity by an enormous imaginary pane of glass. It was only fifteen minutes by car to Salò, but at this elevation, and in this setting of extreme beauty, it seemed we were in some far-off Shangri-la.

The peafowl had drifted down from the olive trees where they slept at night and were strutting around the garden. A lone workman tended to flowers at the garden's south end. I found myself sitting in the coolness beneath the trees, staring back at the great sunlit facade of the main house, a well-ordered elevation of deep casement windows, some balconied, and all flanked by louvered shutters of Tuscan red. Like so many Renaissance buildings the villa owed its aesthetic existence to Vitrivius's *De architectura*.

My mind returned to Piruzzi's manuscript, wondering what discoveries might lie within its pages. The historian in me wanted to sit down with it for days, to savor the lost text. Words hold special importance for someone like myself. They are the keys that unlock cultures, and their interpretation is more valuable than the artifact itself could ever be. And yet, the manuscript was also a priceless artifact. The architect in me wondered what it would be like to just *own* something like the manuscript, to know that it was yours, to have it on your night stand. I thought of what the other architects must be thinking, to know that if they succeeded in the competition, that the manuscript would be theirs. Again I thought of Piruzzi's shrewdness, but in this case I truly wondered if a great design was worth the price that he was offering.

It wasn't long before I rose and turned my thoughts to matters at hand. I thought that as a friend I should gather Richard's things together, in order to return them to the States. I stepped across the garden to his pavilion door and made my way inside. The pavilion had an eerie emptiness to it, as if Richard had just stepped out for a moment and time had stood still. In the bedroom his bed was made, and it hadn't been slept in. In the bathroom I found a damp washcloth, one he had probably used just prior to his death. Above the sink his toothbrush shared a glass shelf with an open tube of toothpaste. Across the lowered lid of the toilet lay the shirt and sweater he had worn the day before. On the floor, his crumpled pair of trousers. I collected and folded the clothes. I then took them, along with his toiletries, into the bedroom. There I collected his wallet and a few other personal items, and took one last look around the room. Something drew me to the bed. It was still made up, but in reflecting upon what I had found in the bathroom, something didn't seem right. I pulled back the bedspread and inspected the sheets. My own sheets had been crisply ironed and perfectly smooth when I had gone to bed the night before. Richard's sheets, however, were ruffled. Either he had sat on the bed at some point, or he had gone to bed prior to going back upstairs.

I climbed to the studio and found a few more things,

mostly personal supplies he had brought with him for the competition. His briefcase was an untidy stuffing of papers, but not the kind of papers that businessmen carry. Drawings mostly—legal pads crammed with the doodles of a uniquely creative hand— ideas for buildings, plans, cartoons, nudes, notes to himself. I took the briefcase and a pair of penny loafers, and piled them by the stairway.

Just then I was startled by the sound of someone coming up the stairs. My eyes rose to greet a woman of about my age, standing at the railing. She was pretty, in a boyish sort of way, with long, sun-soaked arms that contrasted her white linen shirt. Her legs were also deeply tanned, and from beneath a pair of cut-off dungarees, they stretched in sinuous lines down to her huarache sandals. Her hair was dark and silken, and she wore it long. She had the smallish mouth and lean face of a Northern Renaissance Madonna, though her eyes were anything but Madonnaesque. They were the color of a deep yellow rose, and they were the atmospheric eyes of a jaguar. It took me a moment to realize that she was the woman I had seen the day before in the woods.

"I've heard about the death of the American," she said in perfect English, looking around the room.

"It was a complete shock," I said.

"He was one of the architects?"

"Yes. Richard Battle. By the way, I'm Jamie Ramsgill."

I extended my hand, and after a brief hesitation, she grasped it. She had long supple fingers and soft skin.

"My name is Elena," she said.

I studied her closer. Her clothes were simple yet stylish. Her hands were too well kept to be those of a servant.

"Are you Renzo's daughter?" I asked haltingly.

She nodded shyly, a slight hint of a smile rising at the corners of her mouth.

"I'm just collecting some of Richard's things to return to his family," I said. "He was a friend."

"Sorry," she said. "You'll return to America with his belongings?"

"I'm not sure. The family may want them sooner than my return. And I don't know when that'll be."

Her mouth turned down.

"Will Father's contest not be canceled?" she asked.

"No," I said. "The other architects have voted to go on."

She pulled her hand away from the railing and stepped into the studio. She walked lightly, like a cat on soft ground.

"That's surprising," she said. She seemed disappointed. "I would have thought that under the circumstances you wouldn't go on. You architects are a greedier lot than I suspected."

"I suppose we are."

"And so Father still plans to build his monument on the hillside?"

She was walking slowly around the room, her fingers kissing everything within reach.

"Monument?" I asked, my head following her trail.

"Sure," she said, stopping. "He calls it a chapel, but we all know that it's only to be a burial monument for one of the biggest egos in all of Italy."

Her relationship with her father was not particularly a topic I wanted to discuss. I tried to change the subject.

"By the way. Didn't I see you yesterday? In the woods?"

"I'm in the woods most days," she said.

"You were filming something, weren't you?"

"Actually, videotaping," she corrected. "I was video-taping birds."

I awaited an explanation.

"I see you don't understand. It's that I'm studying for a Ph.D. in zoology at Bologna. My project is the study of the indigenous bird habitats."

"Oh? Sounds interesting."

"It is. They're brilliant animals."

"What aspect of them are you studying?"

"Their familial relationships, and the influence of man in and around their habitat. They're endangered because of all of the building around the lake. It's changing very quickly now. The new development is not sympathetic to what's already here."

"Is that really a problem?" I asked.

"Yes. Even Father's insensitive."

"What do you mean?"

"He has plans to put the chapel in an area of important habitat. The birds will have to move on. There's less and less habitat each year."

"Have you talked with him about the placement of the chapel? Seems to me that there are other places on the villa grounds it could go. Without destroying the woods, that is."

"I've spoken to him many times. But he's determined to have it his way. If you don't know him very well, Mr. Ramsgill, you will soon learn that he is very . . . how do you say . . . obstinate."

"Sorry," I said. "As a matter of fact, we all came here thinking that he wanted the architects to design a new headquarters building near Milan. We knew nothing about the chapel."

"Mmh," she said, brushing a strand of hair from her eyes.

"That's just like him, manipulating people that way. Yes. That's very typical. He has no need of a new head-quarters, you see. His interests are no longer with his business."

"No?"

"No. Power is his real game. He only wants that which he doesn't have. Once he has it, he loses interest."

I thought of the Vitruvius manuscript. No telling what he went through to get it. And now, he was willing to give it up to get something else. Something he must want more.

"Your father's an interesting character," I said.

"Difficile is more how I would put it," she said. "But lovable. He's also very rich, of course. If you depend on him, as I do, then you learn to bend to his desires."

I recalled Piruzzi's disclosure to me yesterday that uncontracted power was what he longed for.

"But, I must be going," she said. "I'll let you return to your work." Her lips formed into what appeared to me to be a smile, but it seemed she caught herself, and the smile disappeared.

"Thanks," I said. "And I can see how it must be frustrating for you. Sorry he's so insensitive, but it sounds as though he'll get his 'monument,' as you call it, whether any of us objects or not."

"So he would think," she said. "But I've learned a lot from him. There still may be methods to dissuade."

FIVE

I spent the remainder of the morning making overseas phone calls in as thoroughly unpleasant a task as I'd ever had. With the time difference, I woke Richard's family before dawn with the grim news, which I found especially painful. His ex-wife Eleanor took it calmly. It was as though she had expected it. But his daughter, Chris, broke down on the phone, and I was utterly incapable of soothing her. Her frail voice was weakened by our long-distance connection. I found myself wishing that I'd simply let her mother explain to her what had happened. The more I talked, the less reassuring I sounded, my own feelings about Richard finally coming to the surface. I suppose I was feeling the guilt that others close to an alcoholic must feel when that person slips off the edge, even if it is outside their power to help. In hindsight, it now seemed, Richard had been slipping for years.

After hanging up I ordered lunch in my room, and while waiting, I sat on my balcony and gazed out to the picturesque landscape. In the foreground it was the variety of flora shape and texture that caught my eye: dark rocket-like cypress, billowy umbrella pine, bulbous magnolia, weeping somber hemlock. Beyond, the atmosphere blended the variety into a sameness, with each successive mountain plane softer and more blue. It was the kind of

scene that normally elicits in me a desire to sketch, but
after talking to Richard's family I simply couldn't get
inspired. Lunch soon arrived, a sandwich of Soprassota
and thick aged parmesan, with olive oil on fennel-stud-
ded focaccia. While I ate I recorded in a notebook my
observations of the last twenty-four hours, as Piruzzi had
requested. I then took a look at the competition building
program we had received at breakfast, the program for
the "monument," as Elena had called it. There wasn't
much to it, and I found myself wondering why Piruzzi
was offering such incentive to design this little chapel.

Once finished I decided to make my rounds of the
competitors, to answer questions in my role as advisor. I
started with Thornburgh Keller, my next-door neighbor.

"May I help you?" he asked as he answered his door.
He wore a loose silk shirt and dark slacks, topped by a
light blue seersucker jacket. In his hand he held the competition brief, and he had a pencil tucked behind his ear.

"How are things?" I said. "Piruzzi's asked me to check
on you . . . to see how the competition's going."

"Why me?" Keller snapped.

"Not just you," I replied. "All of the competitors. Do
you mind if I come up and have a look?"

He opened the door wider and motioned me in with an
exaggerated swing of his arm.

"By all means, Professor. If Piruzzi wants you to come
up, then so be it."

I hesitated, sensing the sarcasm in his voice.

"Oh, come on, Ramsgill," he said. "Just kidding. Besides, I've been wanting to talk with you."

I followed him in. We climbed the narrow stairs to his
studio, whereupon he reached his drafting table before
me. On his table was a collection of books and papers,
piled high and competing for space at the table's edge. He
seemed to push one or two of the books aside before I got
there. He then placed some other books on top of those
that he had moved. Finally, he placed his body between
myself and the books.

"As you can see," he said, "I'm just beginning."

Before us on the drawing board was taped some yellow tracing paper, and on the paper, sketched out lightly, was a building plan. It was a deft plan, very geometric, with thick walls and a distinct demarcation between the outer envelope of the building and its spaces within. I was frankly surprised that Keller had produced it.

"Looks promising to me," I said.

He seemed surprised at my comment.

"You think so?"

"Do you have any questions about the program?" I asked. "I'll try to answer them if I can."

"Nothing in particular," he said. "I think I fairly well understand what Piruzzi has in mind."

I again cast my gaze at his drawing. There was something oddly familiar about it, as if I had seen it before. It didn't look like the sort of thing Keller normally did. I turned my attention to the pile of books, and I then realized that one of the books Keller had pushed aside and covered with the others was a monograph. A monograph on the works of Richard Battle. The plan drawing, it now came to me, was a loose copy of the famous chapel Battle had designed fifteen years earlier at Bryn Mawr College. Now that Richard was dead, I guess Keller felt he could replicate it.

"I *was* wondering," Keller said, seeing that my attention was drawn to the monograph, "whether or not the hillside will support conventional building foundations for the chapel. Or will pilings be required?"

The question was meant to divert me. The thing of it was, however, the question illustrated the problem with copying Battle's design. Battle's Bryn Mawr chapel was a building that stood in the center of a relatively flat campus and was meant to be experienced from all sides. Piruzzi's chapel was to be tucked into a steep hill, hard against the walls of the villa. Now that I thought of it, Keller's attempt to make Battle's building fit his purpose was extremely naive. I felt sorry for him, especially if he was as desperate as Richard had said he was.

"On page four of the program," I said. "Under 'Structural Remarks,' it's clear from the first paragraph that piles will be required."

He picked up the program and nervously rifled through it.

"Oh yeah. Guess I missed it. Quite stupid of me."

He looked down at his plan.

"I guess this *parti* doesn't make much sense on such a steep site," he said.

I didn't want to shoot him down, but I didn't want to encourage plagiarism, either.

"I don't think I'm supposed to critique that way. Piruzzi wants me to be an objective advisor. With all of you."

He set down the program and walked to the window. He stood for a moment gazing out to the garden, then he spoke.

"How are the others doing?" he asked.

"Actually, you're the first I've talked to."

He turned his head in my direction. I sensed he wanted more information.

"Look," I said. "Even if I had talked to the others, Piruzzi wouldn't want me to tell you anything. You know how he is about rules."

He looked at me silently. He then removed his glasses and retrieved a handkerchief from his jacket pocket. His deepset eyes were red. With his glasses off he looked like a much older man.

"I suppose," he said solemnly. "Very mysterious, this Piruzzi. I really don't see the need for all the secrecy."

"It's a competition, Thornburgh."

"Yeah."

"By the way," I said, "what was it that you wanted to talk to me about?"

"Nothing important. I was just interested in your opinion of the Vitruvius manuscript." He returned the glasses to his nose. "Do you think it's real?"

"It appears to be," I said.

"Where would you get something like that?"

"No telling. It could have been stashed away in a church somewhere, or a library."

"But it's one of a kind?"

"Put it this way. If it took five hundred years for a single copy to surface, then it's a pretty safe bet we're talking about something unique."

"It must be terribly important. I suppose it's worth a lot of money."

"A *lot* of money," I said.

He stared at me again, in silence.

"Ramsgill," he finally said. "Have you heard the stories going around about my financial troubles?"

"I've heard rumors."

"Well, unfortunately they're not rumors."

"Sorry."

"Don't be. I've accepted it, and I'll live with it. But that doesn't mean I won't claw back to solvency. Somehow."

"And a priceless manuscript would help, wouldn't it?"

"I'll do whatever it takes to win."

"I'm sure you will."

"Whatever," he repeated.

I let it drop.

"Ramsgill, are you happy in your teaching position?"

"Very."

"You're tenure track, aren't you?"

"Yes."

He stepped away from the window and came towards me.

"Tenure would mean a lot to a young faculty member like yourself, wouldn't it, Ramsgill? You do want to stay at Princeton, don't you?"

He was standing in my face. He looked up at me through his thick glasses.

"What are you driving at, Thornburgh?"

He wanted something from me. I didn't know what,

but when someone as powerful and as driven as Thornburgh Keller starts showing concern for little old me, he isn't doing it out of the kindness of his heart.

"Jamie, I know every tenured professor in your department. Your department chairman used to work for me. And I'm on the Board of Overseers at the school. What I'm leading up to is that I might just use my influence for you, if for any reason you want it . . . you know . . . to help you along."

"You mean when I come up for tenure?"

"Yes."

"No thanks. I'll make my own way."

"Jamie, all I want is a little information."

"Such as?"

"Such as keeping me informed as the competition goes along. You know, what the others are doing, what Piruzzi's thinking, that sort of thing."

"I can't do that, Thornburgh."

I stepped away from him. I didn't like being stared at.

"Very well, Ramsgill."

"I think I should move on," I said nervously.

"As you wish," he said.

He motioned towards the stairs and followed me down to the front door. I stepped out into the garden and felt like an uncaged bird.

"I'll be going, then."

"Ramsgill, I hope you might reconsider my offer."

"Sorry, Thornburgh."

He adjusted his shirt and jacket cuffs and thrust his chin forward in a patrician manner.

"It is I who am sorry. Sorry for you."

"What are you talking about?" I said. My voice now had a perceptible edge to it.

"I described the influence I have at the university," he said. "That influence can be used two ways, you know."

"You wouldn't," I said angrily.

"Wouldn't I? I've told you what this competition means to me."

"That's blackmail, Keller."

"Call it what you wish, Jamie. Now won't you reconsider? Or do you want your career up in smoke?"

I started to speak, but I thought it better to contain my profanities. The bastard wasn't worth wasting my breath on. In silence I turned and left him standing at the door.

Fifteen minutes later I was still seething. Before this weekend, I had known Keller only by reputation, but now, having seen him in action, he was every bit the jerk I had heard he was. I wondered if he would follow through on his threats. I wondered too whether my colleagues at the university could be swayed by him. It was no secret that I had problems with some of the old-guard faculty. Most young teachers do. Several of them had seen to it that my tenure vote be postponed indefinitely. And if Keller did wield power within the school, then it was probably with that particular faction.

I considered telling Piruzzi of the episode but decided to let it pass. I resigned myself to quiet indignation, and after cooling down I made my way over to Pet Clissac's pavilion to check on her progress.

She was well out of the blocks, working frenetically amid the swirls of cigarette smoke, smoke that formed a haze in the upper reaches of the studio, near the ceiling. Mounds of sketches on crumpled yellow tracing paper invaded all corners of her table, and between them, like a flat clearing in a forest, her bold plan stretched across the front of the drawing board. Her design looked like anything but a chapel, an obfuscated eruption of slicing planes and soaring towers, stitched together by cage-like framework. She drew frantically with a wide-tipped Magic Marker, the black ink from it flooding the page. Though cordial, she was decidedly uninterested in slowing her hurried pace, if only for a few moments, to enlighten me regarding her design. I probably wouldn't have understood it anyway. Knowing the momentum it takes to follow a lead when you think you are on to a design, I stayed but a few minutes before leaving her and walking across to Gio Borromini's pavilion.

Once there, I considered whether Borromini would even be inside. When he stormed off earlier because of Piruzzi's offering the Vitruvius manuscript as a prize, I thought perhaps that he had left the villa for good. But a moment after knocking, the door opened and a slightly disheveled Borromini answered. He was just finishing off a container of yogurt, scraping the bottom of the cup with his spoon to collect the last little bit.

"Good afternoon," I said.

"Hello, Jamie. How are you?"

I told him my reason for being there. Without hesitation he invited me up.

"Can I get you something to eat?" he said, once we had arrived. "Or a drink?"

"No, I won't be long. I just want to see how it's going . . . and, well, frankly . . . I wasn't sure after this morning that you'd still be here."

He eased his angular frame into an armchair and clasped his attenuated hands behind his head.

"I thought about quitting," he said. "But you know, Piruzzi's right, the shrewd bastard. If I want to make sure that *De architectura* remains in my country, then I'd better win the competition. It's the only choice I have."

I appreciated his pragmatism.

I then glanced over at his drawing table, which, though cluttered with drawings like Pet Clissac's, presented a strangely anachronistic scene. Whereas Clissac's drawing table had been outfitted with the latest hardware and high-tech halogen drafting lamps, Borromini's table was illuminated by a single brass oil lamp, one that he must have brought with him to the villa. The lamp struggled to cast a faint undulating light upon his drawing surface. The drawings that lay there were not executed upon yellow tracing paper, but rather—as I should have suspected, knowing Borromini and his penchant for the past—upon stiff rippled parchment paper, torn and irregular at its edges. The drawings were executed with a long quill pen, which rested upright in a crystal inkwell. Alongside the inkwell were several chiseled pencils made of soft stone. An antiquated T-square lay across an ordered classical plan—Borromini's design for the chapel, no doubt. A pile of sketches on parchment lay next to the plan, vignettes of phantasmagoric machines, the kind of thing Leonardo da Vinci produced in the fifteenth century. Beyond the sketches a pile of source books lay— Andrea Palladio's *I quattro libri dell'architettura*, Sebastiano Serlio's *Tutte l'opere d'architettura*, Leon Battista Alberti's *Della Pittura* and Morgan's contemporary translation of Vitruvius.

I picked up one of the Leonardesque sketches.

"What are these?" I asked.

He rose and came to my side.

"They're my designs for heating and cooling the chapel," he said.

The chapel, of course, meant Piruzzi's chapel, though if I hadn't known Borromini and his work, I would have thought that the sketch before us was something from another century. The drawing seemed to be the heating detail. It was a sectional perspective drawing of the building, with the equivalent of primitive solar collectors on the roof. According to notes on the drawing, the collectors were made of large slabs of black granite set beneath glazing made up of layered oil cloth. The slabs were pitched to the incline of the roof, with what appeared to be a hydraulic piston to force water vertically within the walls of the chapel. According to the drawing, the water, in turn, would cascade across the granite, absorbing heat and being collected in a trough before being funneled via gravity back down within the walls and under the floor. The heat would be dissipated through a masonry tile floor.

"Interesting," I said. "Solar panels from . . . oh, the fifteenth century, I'd guess. You truly refuse to use anything modern, don't you?"

He smiled at the sketch before him. "I have no reason to," he said, "and I have every reason to use traditional methods."

"Why?"

He thought for a moment while he tidied up the stack of sketches.

"Well, it's easier on the environment, for one," he finally said. "You can tell that, no doubt, from this very simple system. And traditional methods employ workers, not machines. It keeps the populace employed. But most importantly, I suppose, it makes the entire building process cooperative. Every person working on the project is involved in the design, the details. Modern construction is nothing but the equivalent of factory work. Each man does but a single task. Lay five hundred bricks in a day. Solder copper pipes. Caulk the joints around windows. And so on. With my buildings the workers are craftsmen, and they're involved in every aspect of the work. They love what they do and therefore my buildings are a product of love. It shows."

"That's fine, Gio, for people who can afford it."

"What's not to afford? Is a man on the state welfare not more costly than putting someone to work?"

There was some logic to his notion.

I stared again at the heating sketch.

"But where do you draw the line?" I asked. "I mean, in this sketch, for instance, wouldn't you need a mechanical pump to get the water to the roof? How would you power it without electricity?"

He smiled.

"There are several ways," he said. "Animals could do the work, for instance, or men. Maybe a hydraulic ram. Or as at the Villa Lante, gravity from a higher water source might do."

I thought of his characterization of his workers as craftsmen. I wouldn't exactly call hand-cranking a water pump all day skilled labor. It seemed he had fallen into the trap of skewed logic that underlies most radical ideologies, from communism to trickle-down capitalism. The sacrifice of one part of the system for another.

"It's interesting," I said. "I can't say that I'm sold, but I appreciate what you're trying to do."

I then took him up on his offer for something to drink. We continued talking while he worked, sharing ideas and discussing theoretical points. He was generous with his time, and I left him, if not with full respect for his archaic approach to contemporary architecture, at least with an understanding of the sincerity and rigor with which he applied his craft.

Next, I knocked on the door of Sir Colin Garbutt, who called from his studio for me to enter. When I arrived at the loft I found him sitting deep within an oversized armchair that was outfitted in a floral Jacquard of midnight blue. He was puffing on an ivory pipe, and he stared off to the landscape through an open window, much as I had during my lunch.

"Ramsgill," he said without looking my way. "Join me in my stoicism."

The aroma of pipe tobacco floated my way, a smell similar to that of cinnamon, or some other combination of spices.

"What's the matter?" I asked.

"This bloody Italian. What does he think he's doing?"

I pulled up a ladder-backed chair and sat next to him. His skin exuded warmth and his body a sweetness. He was somebody you felt comfortable with, like a grandfather.

"You mean Piruzzi?"

"Of course I do," he said.

"You're still upset about the chapel program?"

"I am," he replied, turning to me with deliberateness.

"Not to offend you," I said, "but I think it's pretty shrewd of Piruzzi to do what he did. As he said, it ensures that the competition will be fair. No one gets a head start."

He raised an eyebrow and slid his tongue across teeth

so perfect that they had to be dentures. They were almost
the color of his pipe.

"You're his advisor," he said. "What does it hurt him
if the competitors have been thinking ahead of time?
Doesn't that ensure a better building? It's insane to design a building in two days."

"We all knew there would be rules before we came," I
said. "This is sport to him. Why else would he offer a
prize like the Vitruvius? The building is secondary."

"May well be. But I don't appreciate it. It's like pre-
paring to run a marathon in a track and field meeting,
but once there finding that you've been chosen for the
pole vault. I just don't understand it."

"So what are you going to do?" I asked.

"What else can I do? I'm surely not going to quit. He's
got us by the balls, as you Yanks would say."

I chuckled. He leaned forward and relit his pipe with
a deftly struck wooden match.

"Have you begun?" I asked. "I'm supposed to bring
Piruzzi up-to-date tonight."

"Heavens no," he said, his head now surrounded by
puffs of swirling gray smoke. "One has to think about
these things. Can't bolt like the mare's foal."

"I guess not."

"What are the others up to?" he asked.

It seemed that everyone was concerned with his competition.

"Borromini and Clissac are working hard. And the
others I haven't seen yet."

"I should have expected that the younger generation
would be off quickly."

"The *younger* generation?" I said. "You're not so old,
Sir Colin."

He looked my way with a warm smile.

"I'm last decade's news, old boy, surely you know
that. Why on earth Piruzzi invited me to this affair I
haven't the foggiest. Clissac and Borromini have gim-
micks, and I don't have one. It's like the emperor's

clothes. Clissac has her French Deconstructivism, what-ever the hell that is. An architectural style patterned after literary theory. Jolly ridiculous. And then there's Borromini, with his historic revival. As relevant in today's world as the steam locomotive."

The words *steam locomotive* rolled off his tongue with the wonderful rhythms of the Queen's English. A British stage actor could hardly have spoken them better.

"I guess you're not too fond of Clissac after what she wrote about your Office of Foreign Affairs," I said.

"Clissac's a horse's ass, like most of her countrymen. What has she ever built? Two or three houses, a couple of apartment renovations? That's dilettante fare."

I didn't answer. I waited for him to say something else, but he went back to staring out the window and puffing on his pipe.

"So you don't want to talk about the chapel?" I finally asked.

"Tell Piruzzi I'm brooding," he said, staring straight ahead. "I won't let him down, though."

"I suppose I should be off then," I said. "If you do get started and have any questions, don't hesitate to call. That's what I'm here for."

I was beginning to wonder what I really *was* here for. I had certainly not given any advice in my first few hours of the competition.

"I will," he said rising with aged motion. "I'll be over my bout of depression shortly, and maybe I'll show the younger set that the old man still has some life."

I excused myself and then made my way over to Akio Hara, the last of the competitors. He stood in stocking feet before me at the door with a sweater draped over his rounded shoulders. His eyes squinted as he gazed out into the afternoon sunlight. He looked tired.

When I reached his studio I understood why.

"And I thought the others were off to a good start," I said.

He smiled and looked at his handiwork. A man in his

late fifties, who probably had not built a model with his own hands in decades, had constructed in but a few hours a large-scale contour model of the site, using his limited materials to great advantage. It was covered with a sort of papier-mâché and brushed with impressionistic tempera to give it a realistic effect. Beside it, stuck into cardboard, was a forest of scaled trees, so real that I could almost smell their foliage.

"I wanted to get the model out of the way," he said. "Too often I see my students in Tokyo design good buildings but not leave themselves enough time to finish their presentation. By constructing the model first I can now devote the rest of my time to design. It also helps me think about the chapel as I build. It gives me a sense of the natural world from which the building will grow. A building should be in harmony with its environment."

I considered the sincerity of Hara's approach compared to Keller's. This, I thought, is how design should be.

"Very nice," I said. "And I expect that your building will be every bit as beautiful. Do you have any questions about the *dottore*'s program? Do you understand it?"

I was worried that the program, which had been translated into English from Italian, might be a difficult read for a Japanese.

"My English, while not perfect, serves me well," he replied.

He started inserting the completed trees onto the model landscape, carefully gluing them into place one by one.

"Your English is as good as mine," I said. "Did you just pick that up over the years?"

He smiled a slight smile. "Oh no. I lived in America."

"You did?"

"Yes, during graduate school. Nineteen fifty-four to fifty-seven."

"I didn't know," I said. "Where'd you go to school?"

"Yale."

It then occurred to me that Hara must have overlapped with Richard at some point.

"You weren't in school with Richard, were you?" I asked.

"Oh yes. We were in the same class."

"I never knew that," I said.

"Yes, Richard and I surely competed for every prize and scholarship that the school gave out during our time there. He, as the American, I think, won the most. The school was not so equitable to its overseas students, especially the Japanese. This was not so many years after the war, you understand."

I nodded. His mind seemed to linger on his school days.

"I was very interested to learn that Richard would compete here," he then said, "to give me another chance to better him."

"But now you won't have your chance."

"No. I'm very sorry about what has transpired, my envy from our school days notwithstanding. You must be very sad too."

"It's okay," I shrugged. "In a funny way my real grief is for the fact that Richard's ideals will die with him. See, he believed that architects have lost their values. That design has become fickle . . . an ephemeral game. Too much hype. He wanted to build, not play games."

Hara placed his last tree on the model. He then walked to the sink and began washing his hands.

"I can appreciate that," he said. "But you know, Jamie, as well as I do, that one has no choice but to play games today. It's changed from when Richard and I first started out."

"In what way?"

"Well, the public doesn't know much about architecture, do they? In general they rely on what they learn from the media. The media—at least the part of it that even pays attention to architecture—builds up a select few designers. It creates stars, personalities that are better known than buildings. Each of us here is considered a star. But I also believe that I'm a good architect. And if you believe your work to be good, then I think you must sell yourself, as well as your buildings. You must take every advantage to get the job, and once you get it, you must take every advantage to make people think that it is brilliant. There are some very well-known architects that have little talent. But they're masters at public relations."

I thought of Thornburgh Keller, and the games that he played. But Hara was right. And he *was* a great talent. He only played games because he felt it a prerequisite in today's profession. Talent alone is indeed not enough, witness the demise of Richard's career.

"So you see," he said, drying his hands. "We must all do what we can to get ahead. Success is never guaranteed."

I stared at him for a moment before he returned to work. He moved to his drawing table and began sketching on yellow trace, once in a while casting a studied gaze back to his model. From time to time he would look up and make a comment to me, but he was not going to stop what he was doing to discuss the finer points of the architecture profession. I respected him for that and excused myself, making my own way back downstairs. As I walked through the garden I continued to think about what he had said. He was an engaging personality and I found myself pondering the subject of how far an architect would go to succeed. Now that the competition was rolling, each of the competitors was approaching the problem in a different manner, each at his or her own pace. It would be fascinating to watch the outcome, what it would take to win the priceless manuscript, not to mention Piruzzi's commission.

I ambled over to one of the stone balustrades that separated the garden terrace from the outside world. I was thinking of how Piruzzi had set up an elaborate game of chess within the confines of our little world. The

competition, through inviting the world's most renowned architects and offering them priceless compensation, was as full of hype as any game that could be
conceived. And yet Piruzzi had gone to great lengths to
ensure a fair competition. This was an interesting dichot-
omy, and given time, it just might separate the men from
the boys, as it were. Unless Piruzzi was entirely capri-
cious at the end of the weekend, and unless he chose a
scheme for other than meritorious reasons, then there
would be no way for someone like Keller to manipulate
his way in his usual manner to success. The best man, or
woman, would win. Or at least the most resourceful.

SIX

Candlelight danced a minuet on walls of cherry, and a fire crackled in the library's carved stone hearth. While we waited for dinner, I sipped my second glass of dry sherry. The day had stretched to an interminable length, so many hours ago it seemed that I had awoken to find that Richard was dead. The sherry embraced me, as did the room, and I slipped into a dream-like state, the voices of my colleagues drifting in and out of my head.

Akio Hara and Thornburgh Keller stood across from me, the two of them studying the Vitruvian manuscript, which now rested under glass in a heavy walnut vitrine along one of the long walls of the room. They spoke softly, almost secretly, though from time to time Keller's voice rose to an excited intonation. Hara had his nose pressed right up against the glass, and he seemed to nod at Keller's every word. Keller did most of the talking, and I could tell from seeing him now, as well as from our earlier conversation, that *De architectura* held a place of extreme importance in his mind.

Behind me, facing the fire, were Pet Clissac and Gio Borromini. The two of them were sitting on a long settee, and they seemed to be discussing the muralled ceiling above us. Like the ceiling of the dining room, the library ceiling was divided into seven geometric panels. The cornice that Borromini had so admired last night wrapped its way around solid wooden beams, the beams in turn creating deep coffers, within each of which the muralled panels found homes.

In the center was a large circular panel, and within that, a depiction of what appeared to be the Holy Communion. The attenuated figures were painted skillfully in the illuminated style of a Tintoretto. The bright faces of the figures strained to stand out from murky surroundings, murky not because of the painter's choice of colors, but rather because of the painting's age and its need for conservation. The remaining six panels, of various geometric shapes, surrounded the center one, and they were all similarly tarnished.

The scenes were of religious subjects—one a baptism, another matrimony, a third an anointing with oil. As they had been so carefully laid out and made to conform to the number of panels, there was no doubt in my mind that the overall theme was linked directly to the number seven. Clissac and Borromini were speculating on their meaning, though neither could link the subject matter to the number. Nor could I, but there was something familiar about the iconography.

"Jamie," Piruzzi said, sitting in a chair next to me and jarring me from my musing. "How are you, my friend?"

"Not too bad," I said. "Considering the day."

"I want to talk with you after dinner regarding the competition. But alone."

"Fine," I said. "I saw everyone today. Some of them are working quite hard."

"Some of them?"

"Well, it doesn't seem that Thornburgh or Sir Colin have done much. But Hara, for one, has a smashing model."

He smiled, which brought out the roundness of his face.

"We can talk about that later. Were you able to contact Mrs. Battle?"

"Yeah. But she wasn't too upset. She and Richard had been divorced for years, you know."

"I see. Well, I contacted the U.S. authorities about arranging with the family to have the body returned. I assume that the family would like him buried over there."

"Yes."

"Also, as I suspected with our country's bureaucracy, it will take many days before that can be accomplished. In the meantime the body is being held in the *obitorio* in Salò. We have an archaic custom here of keeping the body on marble for twenty-four hours prior to the autopsy."

"If that's the case, then there's nothing we can do but wait."

"Correct."

"I also spoke with the inspector," he continued.

"Have they officially determined Richard's cause of death?"

"Not yet. You have to realize how slowly things are done here. He was going to stop by the hospital at the end of the day. He'll try to get some answers out of Stavalos. He said if he found out anything, he would come up here this evening."

Just then Cavalliere entered the room. He had gone to look for Sir Colin, who was late for dinner.

"Garbutt's door is locked, sir," he said to Piruzzi. "And he doesn't answer."

Piruzzi and I exchanged nervous glances. Clissac and Borromini overheard Cavalliere, and Hara's head popped up from the manuscript case. Piruzzi rose, and we followed him out to the garden. He knocked loudly several times at Garbutt's door, which was just steps from the back terrace.

"Would you like me to get the key, sir?" Cavalliere asked once it was clear that Garbutt wouldn't answer.

I bent over and peered into the lock. It had an old-fashioned hourglass-shaped keyhole into which a key could be inserted from either side. I could see nothing but darkness as I looked in, though from the door's glass transom I knew the foyer to be lit.

"It's locked from inside," I said. "The key must be in the lock."

"A key won't do any good," Piruzzi said. "Franco, could you break the door down?"

Cavalliere was a big man. He took a number of running shoulder thrusts at the door. On the third try the door sprang open and several pieces of wood from the inside door casing exploded across marble foyer floor.

"Garbutt," Piruzzi called, first inside. "Garbutt!"

We made a quick sweep of the downstairs, then followed Piruzzi up to the studio. The room was darkened, with the exception of a toppled lamp that lay on the floor as if it had been swept from a nearby table. It was still lit, however, and its light spread upward towards the sloped ceiling, but before reaching it, the light illuminated the dangling body of Sir Colin, hanging free in the middle of the room. His shadow defaced the ceiling like some surreal wallpaper. A wire was wrapped tight around his neck. His face was sullen and his mouth depressed, and his dentures lay on the plank floor beneath his feet. Everyone stood aghast while I jumped up on a chair and jerked frantically at the wire in an attempt free him. My attempts were to no avail.

"Stop it!" yelled Keller in an irritated voice. "It'll do no good. He's dead."

I stepped down from the chair and Keller removed his fingers from Sir Colin's wrist.

"Franco," Piruzzi said softly. "Telephone the police."

Cavalliere quietly left the room.

"This can't be happening," I said. "What the hell's going on here?!"

Clissac was standing at the typewriter Piruzzi had supplied at each studio desk. She turned on a desk lamp and lit a cigarette. Upon exhaling long and slow, she said, "This is what's happening."

We gathered around and read a typed note that was rolled into the carriage of the machine:

9 August

MY CONFESSION

I have decided to end it all because my career is a fraud. My competition entry for the Office of Foreign Affairs was based upon an idea I thieved from a lesser London designer, who shall remain nameless but to whom I paid a great sum in order that he would go along with my selection as architect. The government has from that day on been my best client, such that my entire practice is built upon the foundation of that poor man's work. I have always had the luxury of hiding behind my junior staff, until I was fortunate, or unfortunate as the case now may be, to have received Piruzzi's letter to participate in this competition. On the draughting table you will find a roll of drawings that I smuggled into the villa. For two weeks now my staff have been hard at work on a scheme for the Piruzzi headquarters building that I was to have used in order to finish, and hopefully win, the competition. Alas, Dr. Piruzzi tricked us, and to his credit those drawings are now worthless. I myself am incapable of producing a satisfactory result on the chapel program. I cannot face the humiliation, so I bid you farewell.

I stepped over to the drafting table and unrolled the drawings referred to in Garbutt's note. There were plan drawings, sections, elevations and ideas of atriums and courts for the headquarters building, all drawn up in pencil in what looked to be the same hand, though much more thoroughly developed than one could ever have believed done in two days by a single person. Each was done with precision, and with the kind of detail that only time can produce.

I shook my head disappointedly and started to roll them up again. It was then that I noticed another drawing, this one taped to the drafting table, seemingly in Garbutt's own hand, a plan for the chapel. It wasn't sophisticated, but as I studied it, it was nothing to be embarrassed about either. It had an old-fashioned beaux arts quality to it, ordered spaces connected by thick walls yet with more modern touches, such as plan elements laid out in forty-five-degree angles, the kind of thing I had come to expect from Sir Colin's second-generation Modernism. Given the fact that Sir Colin had nothing on the chapel when I visited him earlier in the day, I was impressed that he had gotten this far.

"*Peu à peu,*" Clissac said, "he has made a nice design. Not bad, even for Garbutt."

"Could he truly have been so depressed at his beginning here to commit suicide?" Hara asked.

I shrugged.

"I suppose," Clissac said, "he must have thought that his office's drawings for the Piruzzi building would win the competition for him. It was a blow when Renzo announced his desire for a chapel."

"True," I said. "But I saw him late this afternoon and he was resigned to the fact that he would have to tackle the chapel."

"He didn't even finish his drawing," Hara offered.

Hara was right. I hadn't noticed it, but the chapel plan was only three-quarters done. A pencil lay near what appeared to be the last line drafted, a crisp stroke made with a straightedge. About halfway across the page, however, the line began to soften, then suddenly it veered off wildly. Further, his parallel edge, which had presumably aided in drawing the line before it went its errant way, was removed from the table and was lying on the floor. The vinyl-coated stainless steel wire through which a system of pulleys makes a parallel edge function like a

T-square had been removed. It was from this wire, which I knew to be devilishly strong, that Sir Colin hung.

"Unusual," Hara said.

"Why?" asked Piruzzi, visibly shaken.

"Because an architect always finishes a line," Hara replied. "Even if interrupted."

"But he had decided to commit suicide," said Borromini from across the room. "He had no reason to finish what he was working on."

I thought about it for a moment.

"All the more reason," I said. "Someone who commits suicide puts his house in order before doing so. You don't stop a drawing in mid-line because of a spur-of-the-moment decision to end your life, then sit down and compose a lengthy and ordered suicide note."

Piruzzi dropped to a sofa in the corner of the room and shut his eyes. "Read me the note again," he said.

Clissac reread it. It was truly painful to hear it again, especially with Sir Colin's lifeless body suspended overhead. The words were those of a pained individual, more pained than he had let on since our time together. It was true that he had been the loudest voice of protest when Piruzzi changed the program for the competition, but I thought from my meeting with him later, and as evidenced by his drawing of the chapel on the drafting table, that he had put his consternation aside and decided to forge ahead.

As Clissac completed the note, I began to think that Garbutt's change of heart and the errant line weren't the only puzzling things about the death. The suicide note had a queer ring to it, something about the language that I couldn't put my finger on but that just didn't sound right. I walked to the typewriter.

"Thornburgh," I said, enlisting the aid of the only other person in the room to whom English was a first language. "Could you look at this?"

He joined me, and while he read I copied the note onto a blank page of my sketchbook.

"Does something about it strike you as odd? The way it's written, I mean."

"Not particularly," he said in his cool manner. "Wasn't it Daniel Webster who said that suicide *is* confession?"

I persisted: "Nothing strikes you about the wording?"

"No."

Piruzzi looked up at the body and said:

"It's my fault. My changing the program pushed this man over the edge."

"Ridiculous," said Clissac. "You did exactly the right thing."

"The fact that he smuggled drawings in," Borromini added. "That confirms that you were right to change the program."

Piruzzi just frowned. He didn't seem comforted by the comments.

Just then Cavalliere's voice came from across the garden, followed by the hollow sound of rapid footsteps. A moment later he entered the studio with Inspector Anghini, who acknowledged our presence with a quick nod of his head. He went directly to Sir Colin's body.

"It's lucky I was already on my way up here," he said. "I want everyone out."

Piruzzi rose from the sofa.

"Gentlemen and Mme. Clissac," he said in a tired voice, "why don't you return to dinner. Franco, see that things are in order."

Cavalliere began to lead us out but was interrupted by Anghini.

"Just a moment," he said. "Who was the last to see the Englishman alive?"

We looked at each other, shrugs all around.

"I saw him around five o'clock," I said.

"Then I would like to talk to you. Wait downstairs."

I did as I was told and followed the others out, leaving Piruzzi with the detective. I sat on a bench in the garden and watched as a parade of officials arrived and took

over the pavilion. My mind was still not at ease over
Garbutt's suicide note, so I pulled out my sketchbook
and studied my copy of it again. By now it was getting
dark, with just a hint of light in which to read.

The note was dated "9 August" in the European manner, which was logical enough. "MY CONFESSION" is
the way it began, an incriminating choice of words for
something I didn't consider all that unusual. Sir Colin
had not struck me as particularly ethical or unethical, but
the use of other people's ideas is certainly not unheard of
in our profession, nor do I believe it grounds for killing
oneself. Nevertheless, "confession" was the word he
chose, and there was something about it that stuck in my
mind. Had I talked with Sir Colin about a confession?
Had I heard him use the word? I didn't know, but it
seemed that I had encountered it somewhere during my
stay at the villa.

One of Anghini's detectives arrived at the front door to
the pavilion and began piecing together the splinters
from the door frame that resulted from Cavalliere's
breaking in.

I left "confession" and read on. He spelled "draughting," as in "draughting table," the way the English do,
which made sense. I continued. "For two weeks now my
staff..." is what Garbutt had written further down in the
note. That sounded a bit odd coming from him.
Wouldn't a Brit have written "For a fortnight now my
staff . . ."? I couldn't be sure. I've always thought of
myself as having a good eye and ear for the distinctions
of culture, and "For two weeks now" seemed like words
coming from someone else. I then recalled a recent letter
I had received from Sir Colin. I was sure that in it he had
stated "see you in a fortnight at the villa."

I read on. I came across nothing else out of the ordinary, so I started again. The policeman in front of me
was working diligently, and the shadows of the men upstairs moved from time to time across the illuminated
windows. The air was cooling and a breeze rode across

the tops of the dark trees beyond the pavilion. I soon
came upon his abbreviation for *Doctor,* as in "Dr.
Piruzzi," which was abbreviated with a period. The odd
thing about that, I realized, was that the English do not
put periods in such an abbreviation. I read on. The next-
to-last sentence ended with the words "chapel program."
Something unusual about that too. I then realized that
the oddity was the word "program." The British spell it
with two *m*'s and an *e* at the end: "program*me.*"

I looked harder. I tried to picture Sir Colin at the
typewriter composing these words. Could he have written them? The note was neatly typed, double-spaced; it
was not in his own hand. I wondered if the typewriters in
the other pavilions were the same. Suddenly, I realized
that the note could have been typed by anyone; it wasn't
handwritten. And then another totally unconnected
thought. That of Anghini asking if Richard got along
with the other architects. And a third. Richard had
begun to prepare himself for bed, maybe even got into
bed, but he never went to sleep.

"Professor Ramsgill."

It was a second policeman standing at the door, above
and behind his kneeling colleague. He motioned for me
to come in. I slowly closed my sketchbook and made for
the door. I started in, but the detective working on the
door was blocking my way so I stood for a moment on
the porch. He was just completing his reconstruction of
the door frame when I noticed a small splinter of wood
resting on top of the foyer baseboard.

"Excuse me," I said in Italian. "I think you've missed
a piece."

He turned and I pointed out the splinter to him. He
picked it up and started to place it in the area he was
working on. There was no room for it though. The door
casing was completely back together. The splinter was a
natural color, which confirmed that it wasn't part of the
door casing at all. He tossed it out into the garden.

Upstairs, Piruzzi was still at the couch and Anghini

was staring out at the balcony with his arms crossed, a cigarette hanging loosely between his lips. The medical examiner, Stavalos, stood over the corpse, which now lay on the floor. Two assistants were trying to maneuver Garbutt into a long black body bag.

Garbutt's muscles looked more rigid now, but his skin was flaccid, and the marks upon his neck more pronounced. The mark left by the wire that he hung from was a thin dark brown crescent, which ran from just below his larynx up towards each ear. Upon closer inspection I noticed another mark too. This one was lighter in color but about the same thickness, and it ran straight around his neck at about the height of a turtleneck collar.

"Professor Ramsgill," Anghini said, turning as I came in. "Sit down."

"I'd rather stand, thank you."

"As you wish. Could you describe for me your encounter with Garbutt this afternoon?"

I told him of our meeting.

"Would you say that he was despondent when you left him?"

"He was despondent when I came in. By the time I left, though, he seemed resigned to get on with the matter at hand."

"The matter at hand?"

"The competition. He must have started work on it. You can see that from the plan he drew up."

"So it would seem. But he was upset with Dottor Piruzzi's change of the program, wasn't he?"

I glanced at Piruzzi. His face was expressionless.

"He was. But several of the competitors were. Myself, since I don't have the opportunity to win the commission anyway, I thought it was a smart move."

"What time did you leave him?"

"Oh, I wasn't here long. I'd say around five-fifteen."

"And where did you go after that?"

The question caught me by surprise. Why the hell was Anghini interested in where I had gone?

"To my pavilion," I said in a strained voice. "You don't think—"

"We don't think anything at the moment. We're just trying to establish facts. Tell me something else. Did Garbutt see you out?"

"No. I believe I made my own way out."

"Did you lock the door behind you?"

"I don't think so. No, I'm sure I didn't. It's not the kind of door that locks itself. You have to have a key. But wait a minute, I want to know something. Do you suspect that his death wasn't suicide?"

Anghini didn't answer, but his silence weighed heavily on my mind. I looked to Piruzzi, who sat passively, his soft hands crossed in his lap. Something about his face corroborated that he too believed what I was beginning to think. Our eyes shifted to the body bag, where the zipper was being closed over Garbutt's silvery hair.

So many unanswered questions, I pondered, as I watched Sir Colin's body disappear. Two dead men in twenty-four hours, one of them a friend of mine. A suicide note that didn't ring true. A fatal loaf of bread found next to what should have been a non-existent bottle of wine. A priceless manuscript offered as a prize. The jealousy and hidden animosity of the competitors.

I tried to make sense of it all. I turned and looked once more at the suicide note that was still as we had found it in the carriage of the typewriter. I wanted to convince myself that I was wrong.

And then I saw it.

The note was typed with neat two-inch margins on either side of a crisp white page. The carriage of the typewriter was far to the left, and the silver typewriter ball rested on the paper in the margin of the note, only about one-half inch in from the edge of the page. I looked up at the margin settings, and indeed they were set wider than those of the note. The note had not been typed on this typewriter.

My mind raced through the events of the last two days.

It slammed to a stop at my conversation earlier in the day with Akio Hara. He had talked about the idea of playing the game to achieve one's success. I had wondered at the time to what degree the game would be played. It seemed now, as I stared in stunned silence at the suicide note, that the game was being played at the highest level.

SEVEN

"I can tell you," I said to Anghini after I regained my composure, "this suicide note was not written by Sir Colin."

"Why do you say that, Professor Ramsgill?"

I gave him my reasons, ending with the fact that the typewriter margins were set wrong.

"Not to contradict you," he said, "but that's rather conjectural."

"Sir Colin didn't commit suicide," I continued, perhaps too emphatically. "And there's something funny about Richard Battle's death, too."

"Ramsgill!" Piruzzi snapped. "You should be careful in your accusations."

"Let's hear him out, Dottor Piruzzi. Are you suggesting foul play?"

"Yes."

"Then continue."

He caught me off guard, as I really hadn't thought out what I had to say. I paused for a moment, then spoke.

"First of all," I said, "Richard was found dead in his studio, the apparent victim of asphyxiation. Is that the conclusion of the autopsy?"

"Well," Anghini said, staring across the room at Stavalos, then back at me. "The official autopsy report's not finished. But I did manage to get my friend, the good doctor, to verify a cause of death. A piece of bread was lodged in his throat."

"Okay," I continued. "Well, I'm not saying that that isn't the way he died, but something's odd. After you left here today I went back to his pavilion. His clothes were in the bathroom and his toothbrush and washcloth had been used. His bed was not turned down, but the sheets were wrinkled. Now, what would explain his behavior? Getting into bed, then getting out, *and* remaking it?"

Neither of them had an answer. I pressed on.

"Also, and this is linked to what I just said, there's an issue with the wine itself. Why wine? Sir Colin said that that wine bottle was empty. Richard was already in his pajamas. And he was wasted. Do you really think he would have gone back to the library for another bottle? No. If he wanted to drink more—if he were even capable of drinking more—he would have drunk scotch. And then there's the wine stains. The way they covered the back and shoulders of his pajama shirt, he appeared to have been drinking while lying down. Now you could say maybe he did ready himself for bed, then crawled into bed with a bottle and choked while in a semiconscious state. But that isn't what happened. He was upstairs, and there are no wine stains in the bed. I think someone forced that wine upon him to make it appear that he had too much to drink, or perhaps to wash down the bread to make it look more like an accident."

"So," said Anghini. "You're saying that someone forced the bread down his throat?"

"It wouldn't be hard. He was probably passed out, if not near it."

"Interesting," said Anghini. "But a drunk could just as easily have done those things to himself."

"Well, what about the bread at his side?" I asked. "That must mean something."

"It probably means he was hungry."

"Odd choice for a midnight snack," I said.

"Odder choice for a murder weapon," said Anghini.

"Why not just strangle him, if as you say he was passed out?"

"To make it look like an accident," I said. "Look, I talked to Sir Colin after Richard's death. I specifically asked him if Richard had brought bread along with him to his pavilion after they left the library. He said no. Richard did take along an empty bottle of Recioto, he said, but no bread."

"According to Sir Colin," said Anghini. "Who's to say that he wasn't extremely drunk too? Are you so sure that his memory's perfect?"

As he was dead now, we'd never find out.

"What about his death?" I asked. "Don't you think it odd, the suicide note and all? The fact that he didn't finish his drawing?"

"That's circumstantial evidence," Anghini said. "We've looked throughout the pavilion and found no other clues. Not even a fingerprint."

"So you *are* looking for something?" I asked.

"We would investigate any suicide in this manner," he said.

I felt as though I was getting nowhere. Why would Anghini refuse to give me a hint that he too believed as I did?

"But why would Sir Colin commit suicide?"

"Oh really, Jamie," Piruzzi said. "Let's be done with it."

"Ramsgill," Anghini said slowly, looking down at the tattered pad on which he had been keeping notes. "Aren't you forgetting one thing? One very important thing?"

"What?" I said defensively.

"The *dottore* told me how before dinner Cavalliere reported to him that Garbutt's door was locked and that he didn't answer."

"Correct."

"You all then came here and Cavalliere had to break the door down."

"Yeah."

"If as you say, or if as I think you are saying, the Englishman was murdered, then how did the killer get out of the pavilion? The door was locked from the inside. The key was in the lock. It's a dead bolt. The only other way out is from the balcony door, which besides being locked also, would require the killer to negotiate a ten-meter drop to the mountainside below."

I'd have to admit that my heart sank when he said that. The locked door was something I hadn't thought of.

"And another thing, Jamie," Piruzzi said. "Just when was Garbutt supposed to have been murdered? You saw him at around five, and we met for dinner at eight. That only leaves a few hours, and we're talking about a villa crowded with servants and guests. His pavilion is just a few yards from the main house. How did someone get in without being seen?"

"I don't know."

Anghini fired up another cigarette.

"You're upset," he said exhaling. "Your friend has died, and now another man. I can assure you that we're under stress too. Go back to your quarters and get a good night's sleep. See if you still believe this in the morning."

I didn't want to sleep. I felt a headache coming on. I wanted to eat.

"Okay," I said dejectedly.

I heaved a sigh as two of the policemen manhandled the body down the tight stairway.

"I think I'll join the others for dinner."

"Very well," Piruzzi said. "But after that go to bed, huh?"

"By the way," the medical examiner Stavalos said from the other side of the room. "There *will* be an autopsy done on the Englishman's body. That should show convincingly how he died. Don't worry, Professor."

"I won't," I said as I left them, but I knew that I would.

* * *

By the time I reached the house, the others had already eaten and were in the library finishing dessert. I joined them there, and Cavalliere offered to bring me a tray with dinner, which had just been cleared from the dining room table.

"Kind of you," I said. "I'm starved."

"Would you like something to drink? We're having dessert wine, but I could bring you something more appropriate from the cellar if you wish."

"No," I said. "Don't go to the trouble. I'll just have what the others are having. Oh, and Franco, do you have something for a headache?"

He brought me two acetaminophen and a full glass of wine. I took a sip and washed down the tablets. Cavalliere left the remainder of the bottle on the coffee table before me. He tidied up a bit more, then disappeared into the kitchen. The others were quiet, and as they finished up one by one, they left, I figured, to do more work on the competition, even though it would surely now be canceled.

While I waited for my food, my mind wandered, a muddle at this point—exhausted, frustrated, and full of confusing information. I sat back in a plump upholstered chair and my eyes drifted upwards. They landed on the ceiling that Borromini and Clissac had discussed earlier.

It was truly quite beautiful, even in its unrestored state. It was a fusion of painting and architecture in a manner that we today seem incapable of producing. It was more familiar to me now, and though I still couldn't connect the subject matter of the murals to the number seven, I knew that there had to be a connection. What was it, I wondered, that linked it to the dining room ceiling with its seven panels, and to the seven pavilions of the garden? The Renaissance mind, as Richard had said, paid great attention to numerical symbolism. I wasn't so sure that all of the murals in the house were from the sixteenth century, but even if they weren't, numerical symbolism

would have been important in the household of good
Italian Catholics well up until the midnineteenth century.
It was a symbolism that, particularly in the Renaissance
and Baroque periods, pervaded all parts of culture, cross-
ing lines between religion, science, the arts, and philosophy. Richard believed the garden, for instance, to
represent the seven planets because of its proximity to the
dining room, whose murals in turn were a representation
of the heavens. At the time I wasn't sure if I agreed, and
I wondered if the garden pavilions possibly represented
the seven sorrows of the Virgin. Clissac thought they
might represent the seven liberal arts.

What were the other "sevens" of the pre-Enlighten-
ment world? I found myself wishing I were back in my
office at school, because there I could've pulled a book
from the shelf and had the answer in a moment. Wasn't
there something like the seven gifts of the Holy Spirit?
I'm sure that there was, but as I studied the panels overhead I confirmed that these were not based on that subject. I took another sip of wine, which went down
smooth, a velvety wine if ever I had tasted one. Just then
Cavalliere returned with my tray.

He asked if I wanted anything else, then excused himself, saying that he had work to do. As the others had
gone, and in my condition, I could have used his com-
panionship, but respecting his position in the household,
I wished him good night. I then returned my thoughts to
the murals.

Individually, the panels were so familiar, yet as a total-
ity their meaning still escaped me. A single mural each
was painted on one of seven subjects. The first was a
communion showing Christ surrounded by his disciples.
The second was a baptism, seemingly at the shores of the
river Jordan. The third was an anointing of oil, which I
believe in church doctrine is called extreme unction. The
fourth a scene of matrimony. The fifth, an ordination, it
seemed. The sixth? Oh yes, it was a confession. And the
seventh? The seventh I didn't know.

I sliced into a succulent piece of beef and chewed slowly as pink juices filled the bottom of my white china plate. I took another bite and followed it with the wine. The meat was delicious, perfectly marbled and broiled just beyond rare, but it overpowered the dessert wine. Velvet, yes, but this wine was not made to go with beef. Steak needs a heavier wine, I thought. Something concentrated, something with tannins. I wished I had asked Cavalliere for a bottle from the cellar.

I took another bite, then more wine. Tannin. Yes, that's what was lacking. I looked at the bottle of wine on the table and read the label. It was Recioto Amarone, the dessert wine we had drunk the night before.

And then a thought entered my mind. Richard had taken an empty bottle of Recioto with him to his pavilion. I ate a few more bites quickly, each time washing them down with the overmatched wine. I recalled the scent of the wine in the glass on the table next to Richard. I smelled the Recioto in the glass in my hand. They weren't the same.

I ate quickly, trying to pull my thoughts together. Something was wrong with Richard's death, more than I had told Anghini. I returned my gaze to the ceiling. The seven murals were familiar in an awkward way, like a face one knows but without a connecting name. I studied them some more, then my mind shifted back to the wine. And suddenly it came to me.

I set down my tray and leapt from the chair, bounding in the direction of the door. Someone had brought another bottle of wine to Richard's pavilion. I had to talk to Anghini again.

I didn't get far. As I reached the hall and started to turn, I stopped dead in my tracks.

I returned to the library and lifted my eyes back to the ceiling.

"Of course," I said to myself. I banged my head lightly with the palm of my hand in a mocking gesture of my stupidity.

The murals *did* have a symbolic link to the number seven. Not the seven planets, and not the seven liberal arts. Not the seven gifts of the Holy Spirit, either. The ceiling represented the seven sacraments. That's what it was. A lesser-known theme in the art of Catholicism. Matrimony, extreme unction, confirmation, baptism, ordination. Five of seven.

What was the sixth? Confession. Sir Colin's suicide note was entitled "My Confession."

What was the seventh? Communion. Richard had choked to death on bread and wine.

EIGHT

It was dark in the garden as I sprang from the dining terrace and came quickly upon Piruzzi.

"Where are you going, Jamie?"

I was out of breath.

"Anghini. Where's Anghini?"

Piruzzi looked up at me as though I were mad.

"Calm down. You've just missed him. What's bothering you?"

I drew a long breath of cool night air and said in a soft voice:

"I've figured it out."

"What?"

"Richard," I said. "The wine in the glass next to him wasn't Recioto. It was a heavier wine. More like a Chianti."

His nostrils flared slightly. "And what does that mean?" he asked.

"It means that it shouldn't have been a Chianti. The empty bottle on the table was a Recioto, the bottle he had brought with him from the library. But I smelled the wine in the glass. It was a more concentrated wine, more tannic. Where did it come from?"

He shrugged.

"If Richard had wanted something else to drink, he would have drunk scotch. He had a whole cabinet full.

Where did the other wine come from?"

"I don't know," he said.

"And the glass," I continued. "Garbutt said specifically that Richard was cradling an empty bottle when they retired. He made no mention of a glass and there are no wineglasses in the pavilion kitchens."

"So?"

"All of it, along with the broken bread at his side, is linked to the murals in the library."

"What on earth are you talking about?"

"The ceiling of the library. Have you ever studied the murals there?"

"Not that I recall. The villa's full of objects I don't particularly know well."

"It's based on the seven sacraments," I said. "Sacraments that confer a state of grace. In the Catholic church seven are recognized. Matrimony, unction, confirmation, baptism, ordination, confession and communion."

"Yes?"

"Don't you see? The participants of the competition occupy seven pavilions in the garden. Two of the architects have been killed—"

"According to you."

"Garbutt's note was entitled "My Confession." There's a confession scene on the ceiling. And Richard's body was found in the presence of bread and wine—communion! Choked to death by the body of Christ. The killer's using the seven sacraments as a theme. The reason the wine was different is that someone forced more wine on Richard, maybe while he was unconscious, or even dead. That would explain the unusual wine stains."

"Jamie, listen to yourself. That's some fantastic story."

"It's not a story," I said.

He stared at me a full five seconds before speaking.

"The police do not go on bizarre stories about murals and ceilings. That only happens in fiction. You've got to have proof."

"The wine in the glass is the proof. It wasn't Recioto. Do you know if Stavalos tested the wine?"

"I don't. We can call Anghini tomorrow though."

"Tomorrow? Why not tonight?"

He crossed his arms and gave me a sly smile.

"Come now, Professor Ramsgill. Are you afraid? You're not suggesting that there's a murderer on the loose, are you?"

His sarcasm irked me.

"I am," I said solemnly.

He paused for a moment and realized, I think, that I was serious.

"Anghini has had a very trying day, as have we all," he said. "I'm not going to disturb him again. We'll talk to the inspector in the morning."

I still thought that we should contact him before morning, but I didn't know how to do it by myself. I felt like a prisoner in Piruzzi's villa.

"You make the rules," I said in a whisper.

"What was that?"

"Nothing."

"I'm going to bed," he said. "And Jamie, remember: you may or may not be right on this. It's probably an explainable coincidence. As Anghini pointed out to you, no one could have gotten out of Garbutt's pavilion after his death with the door being locked as it was."

I didn't respond.

"Look," he said. "If it'll make you feel any better I'll have Cavalliere ask each of our guests to lock his door. But please don't arouse their suspicions until we can talk to the authorities."

I nodded.

"Good night then," he said. "You should get to bed too. You look terrible."

I gave him a half-hearted smile and said good night.

Once he was gone I realized how cool the night was. Autumn was not far away, and at this altitude, hot days quickly succumbed to chilly nights. A clear black sky draped overhead, like a vast black tent with tiny pin-pricks that let light in where the stars were. The stars hung high and the moon was rising, a thin razor-sharp white crescent that reflected across the cobblestones of the garden. Crickets chirped from somewhere outside the walls of the villa. The tiny lights of a distant ferry crawled across the lake, accompanied by a faint infrequent horn. Surrounding me, lights burned in each of the pavilions, except for Richard's, which left an unintended asymmetry to the formality of the space. I found myself drawn to Sir Colin's door, across the courtyard from Richard's pavilion, to turn out his lights and restore order to our little world.

I was too afraid to spend much time there, so I quickly went about my business. I made a quick sweep of the upstairs studio, which by now had been upset by the police. The suicide note was gone, but I thought that while I had the opportunity, I should type a note on his machine so I could later compare it to the note now in Anghini's possession. I quickly typed a few lines of "My Confession" as I had recorded them in my sketchbook. At first glance the typewriting appeared different from the one found at the scene of the crime, but I couldn't be sure.

After turning out the studio lights I returned to the ground floor foyer. The front door key was still in the lock, and I recalled Anghini's question regarding how the murderer could have gotten out of the pavilion while the key was still in the door. He had said that the only other way out was from the bedroom balcony and that such an exit was impossible. To test his hypothesis I walked to the bedroom. Unlocking the French doors there, I stepped outside.

The breeze off the lake was steady now, and the flutter of leaves and the sway of branches were almost all I could sense of the mountainside. My eyes adjusted slowly to the black, then to my right, the rear of Borromini's pavilion came into view. His lights were burning, but I couldn't see him at work there. I returned my gaze to the woods and looked below me into the darkness. It was hard to judge distance, but I could tell that Anghini was correct in that it was too far down for someone to have left the pavilion from the balcony. Borromini's balcony was too far away for someone to have escaped to, and besides, Anghini had said that the balcony doors were locked when he had arrived.

How had the killer escaped? Was I wrong after all? I stood thinking in silence, when suddenly I heard something from back inside the pavilion. I froze. It was the sound of the doorknob turning. The foyer door opened slowly and a bare arm reached in. The foyer light suddenly went out and I was plunged into blackness. The door pulled to and I heard it being locked from the outside.

For a moment I didn't know what to do. It was then that I realized it must be Cavalliere locking up for the night.

"Hey!" I called.

A moment passed. The door opened again and the foyer light came back on. Cavalliere peered down the corridor toward the bedroom. I stepped inside, closing the balcony door behind me.

"It's me," I said. "Jamie Ramsgill."

"Professor Ramsgill. *Mi dispiace.* The *dottore* has asked me to secure all the pavilions. What are you doing here, if you don't mind my asking?"

I approached him. He had changed from his tuxedo and now wore a tight knit polo shirt and jeans. His biceps were tremendous and his forearms rock solid.

"I was just turning out lights too," I said. "And thinking about Sir Colin's death."

"The *dottore* tells me you think Sir Colin was murdered."

"Yeah. The only thing I can't figure out is how the killer got out of here."

"The door was locked from the inside," he said. "We broke it down, remember?"

I nodded. I ran my fingers over the area of door casing that had been reconstructed by one of Anghini's men.

"Do you have the key?" I asked.

"Yes. I was going to return it to the house."

He produced it from his pocket and twirled it between two blocky fingers.

"Is there a special place in the house that keys are kept?"

"In the pantry. I have a cabinet there for such things."

"Who has access to that room?"

He looked at me inquisitively. He had warm eyes, the sad warm eyes of a basset hound.

"Why do you ask that?" he said.

"Just wondering."

"Myself and the *dottore*. We're the only ones who can get into that room."

"Mmh," I mumbled.

"I know what you're thinking, Professor. That the *dottore* or I could have gotten a key to this pavilion. But you're wrong. There's not a separate key for each pavilion. The same key fits all, and there's one in the front door of each pavilion—"

At this I opened my mouth to speak.

"—but," he continued, sensing my eagerness, "with a key on the inside of the locked door turned a quarter turn, a second one cannot be inserted from the other side. That's how you secure the door, given the fact that other people have keys that fit that lock."

He illustrated his point by putting Sir Colin's key into the door on the foyer side, turning it part way, then trying to place another similar key that he had on a key ring into the lock on the garden side. It wouldn't go.

"So you see, Inspector Anghini was right. The door was locked from the inside. No one could have gotten out."

I turned Sir Colin's key in the lock. The lock was well

oiled and it moved the dead bolt without much force being put on the ring at its end.

"I guess you're right," I said.

I removed the key and gave it back to him. I then knelt down and examined the door and its casing again. It looked intact and normal. Except for one thing. There was the faintest, thin dark line rubbed into the edge of the door itself that angled up towards the keyhole. It looked as though it had been made by pressure of some sort. I looked at the outer edge of the door. It too was marred.

And then I had an idea.

"Excuse me," I said. Cavalliere stepped aside.

I walked out towards the bench I had sat on earlier while waiting to be questioned by Anghini. I searched around the bench, then knelt and searched in a flower bed.

"What are you looking for?" Cavalliere asked.

"A piece of wood," I said. "About four centimeters long."

He joined me, and the two of us crawled around on the damp ground.

"Is this it?" He pulled something from the brush.

It was a small squared-off piece of natural wood about an inch and a half long, not much thicker than a matchstick.

"Yeah. Great. Now, do you have any string?"

"There should be some up in Garbutt's studio," he said.

I asked him to go get it while I inspected the door again. A couple of minutes later I showed him what I had devised.

I placed the key in the lock on the inside of the door, just the way it had been when we broke in. I then slipped the wood into the oval, ring-like thumb-turn at the end of the key, perpendicular to the shaft and in such a way that the wood could act as a lever to rotate the key. I loosely looped a string about eighteen inches long around the wood, then as we both stepped outside, keeping tension on the string, I closed the door until it clicked, careful to pull the opposite end of the string with me.

"If I'm right," I said, "this should lock the door."

I gave the string a tug, but nothing happened. I tried again, pulling harder. This time I heard the sound of the bolt being thrown as the wood on the opposite side turned the thumb-turn and rotated the key. When the lock was engaged, I heard the wood fall onto the marble floor, and I pulled the string through the crack between the door and frame free to our side of the door.

"That does it," I said.

"And the force of the string rubbed that groove into the edge of the door," Cavalliere said. "That's very clever."

"That's how our killer got out of here while still leaving the key in the door as we found it. He pocketed the string and no one would have ever known. Only the wood remained in the foyer. It was the wood that I had seen earlier tonight. Apparently it had fallen onto the baseboard. I thought it was part of the door casing."

Cavalliere smiled.

"So you really believe the two gentlemen were murdered," he said.

"I do."

The smile left his face. He stepped closer to me.

"Who do you think did it?"

"I haven't thought that through," I said. "But now that I've proved the door could be locked from the outside, Inspector Anghini will have to listen to me."

"It could be any one of us," he said.

I hadn't put it into perspective, my mind having been so busy dreaming up the scenarios for the killings. The fact that there was a murderer in our midst made it all the more real, and I frankly didn't want to think about it. That's what the police are paid for. On the other hand we were isolated here, and it would be at least until tomorrow before I could talk to Anghini. I suddenly felt uncomfortable in Cavalliere's presence.

"I suppose it could," I said a bit nervously. I cleared my throat and said: "Well, you must have work to do."

His eyes refocused and he glanced off to the garden.

"Yes," he said nodding methodically. "I must tell the others to lock their doors."

"Good night, then."

"Buona notte."

He stepped away and began in the direction of Borromini's pavilion next door. I passed him, walking towards my own pavilion, which in the context of what I now knew seemed a long way from the house, perched out alone at the edge of the dark mountain.

"Professor," Cavalliere called, as I passed him, while he rapped lightly on Borromini's door. "I don't have to tell you to lock *your* door, do I?"

I laughed softly. "It's as good as locked."

I tossed and turned, and turned some more, but no matter how hard I tried I couldn't fall asleep. For some reason I kept thinking about Vitruvius's *De architectura,* the ten books on architecture with their multitudinous chapters—chapters with titles like "Harmonics"; "On Symmetry: In Temples and in the Human Body"; "The Ornaments of the Orders"; and so on. I soon found myself staring up into nothingness, the slightest reflection of the bronze crucifix on the wall above my bed seeming like a lighthouse beacon, working against my tired eyes. I switched on the table lamp and stared at my watch. It was almost two A.M. My throat was dry and I still had a headache. I went to the refrigerator and poured myself a glass of milk, but on second thought, I dumped it into the sink. I quickly put on a robe and made my way downstairs. Two minutes later I was in the living room of the main house, where I got a bottle of vodka from the bar. I returned to my pavilion and fetched a glass, then crawled back under the covers with both glass and bottle.

In a few hours I could tell what I had learned to the inspector, but knowing his skepticism it wouldn't be an easy sell. In a small town like Salò, he had probably not seen violence of this sort, certainly not on the villa grounds of Salò's most famous citizen. He would resist acceptance of the murders, as would Piruzzi, the news being the kind of thing that the tabloids would devour. From New York to Fleet Street to Naples the headlines would be brutal: DOUBLE MURDER AT BIL-LIONAIRE'S VILLA and SHOCK DEATHS IN ITALY. Not the kind of publicity Piruzzi had intended when he invited us here.

Publicity aside, the more difficult question was, Who had murdered our colleagues? It hadn't been clear from the outset that murder was involved, and as Richard's death appeared to have been an accident, Anghini had probably let the opportunity for gathering clues slip away. An autopsy had been performed, but I wasn't sure that a window of opportunity hadn't passed. With Sir Colin's death it had been somewhat different. Anghini and his men seemed in earnest about their investigation, but as he had already told me, they hadn't much to go on, not even a fingerprint.

How to discover the murderer, then, with a dearth of clues? I pondered this question. Though I wasn't sure how a real-life police investigator worked it, I did know something about how fictitious detectives operate. *Ratiocination* is the high-brow term Poe gave to Dupin's method of analytical reasoning. Conan Doyle's Holmes employed a similar method of deduction. Even Vitruvius hinted at a deductive method in *De architectura*. The method, to be exact, involved building an entire picture of something from a collection of seemingly unrelated fragments.

I unscrewed the cap of the liquor bottle and poured myself a drink. I knocked back half of the clear liquid in a single gulp.

In Vitruvius's case, a whole chapter is devoted to the classical notion of symmetry. Symmetry that is not the idea of biaxiality, which is our understanding of the word, but rather, for the ancients, a certain correspondence in nature of the parts of an organism to the whole. In Vitruvius's chapter, he describes the parts of the human body as proportionally related to one another. For example, he writes that the face, as designed by nature, is one-tenth the measurement of a man's height. Also, the length of the foot is one-sixth the height of a man. The other members, too, have their own symmetrical proportions, and it was through employing them that the famous artists of antiquity attained their renown.

His most famous example of symmetry is what came to be known as Vitruvian man. He writes in the book that if a man stretches his arms straight out horizontally from his body, and if a circle is drawn with its origin at the man's navel, then the circle will inscribe the man's body perfectly: from the bottom of his feet to the top of his head, including his outstretched arms. This image, as engraved in the fifteenth century by Leonardo da Vinci, among others, became the symbol for the Renaissance.

Vitruvius goes on to write that symmetry should also govern the design of temples. The rules, he states, have been laid down by Hermogenes, and they have been employed with good effect on the great temples of antiquity. He gives examples. With the Doric order, for instance, the height of a column should be six times its diameter, because the Doric represents man. With the Ionic a proportion of eight to one, more slender, like the female body. The entablature above a column should also conform to symmetrical proportion, as well as the frieze within the entablature. The triglyphs within the frieze should also correspond, the guttae within the triglyphs, and so forth down the line. In fact, Vitruvius goes so far as to state that if a person finds but a fragment of a Doric temple, then by knowing the rules of symmetry, he should be able to reconstruct the temple intact.

As I stared ahead into my faintly lit bedroom, I wondered whether I could construct a solution to the mystery shrouding Richard's and Sir Colin's deaths, armed only with the fragments of data that lay before me. Without hard evidence, it seemed the only way to approach it would be to establish motives for the killings and the times of death, which in turn might help establish who the murderer was.

First there was the time of death. If Sir Colin's testimony could be believed, Richard died sometime after one-thirty in the morning, the time at which he retired. The body was found by Cavalliere at a little before five. A three-hour time frame in which the killer had his opportunity. I tried to picture it in my mind's eye.

More than likely, the murderer found Richard in a state of total inebriation. He must have been passed out in the bedroom, because he had already dressed for bed and the sheets were wrinkled. Perhaps he was still clutching the wine bottle. He probably put up little, if any, fight, and the whole affair couldn't have taken long to complete. The murderer undoubtedly choked him to death, but had to make it look like an accident. He had to be dragged upstairs, but that wouldn't have been difficult, as Richard weighed little more than 140 pounds. The bread was placed at his side, but an empty bottle would have looked suspicious. So the killer decided to get another bottle. Where did it come from? I picked up my sketchbook from the night stand and jotted this down. And the glass? I made a note to myself to talk to the household staff and perhaps take a look at the wine cellar.

I took another belt of vodka and felt a tingling in my spine. My muscles were beginning to loosen, and I hoped that the pounding in my head would soon subside. I shifted my attention back to my pad, once again considering the wine.

Regardless of where the other wine came from, I thought, the murderer then had to force it upon him to make it look as though the choking was an accident. There was then the second bottle of wine to get rid of. The Recioto bottle was left on the table, but the killer would have had to hide the second bottle. Where did it end up? In any event, the whole process couldn't have taken more than an hour.

On the other hand Sir Colin's death was more complex and, as Piruzzi had said, occurred at a time of day, between a little after five and eight o'clock, when it would have been difficult for the murderer to get in and out of the pavilion without being seen. Someone had entered the pavilion quietly, then either surprised him and killed him right away, or engaged him in conversation and then killed him. In the latter case it would have been someone known to Garbutt, and to whose presence he would not have objected. It was true that Garbutt's hearing was bad, and that if indeed he had been at work at his drafting table, someone could have sneaked up on him.

I then recalled the errant line on his drawing board. He undoubtedly was surprised by the murderer. But how was he disarmed? I remembered that there were two sets of marks on his neck, about the same thickness. One appeared to be that of the hanging wire, but there was another one, horizontal. The horizontal mark must have been the mark of strangulation, made by the murderer as he sneaked up on Sir Colin from behind. Another wire was used, because Sir Colin's own parallel edge wire had been the hanging wire. Where had the other wire come from?

Sir Colin was then hung even though he probably was already dead, hung to make it look like suicide. It would've taken someone strong to do it, or perhaps the murderer had an accomplice. The murderer probably then planted the suicide note, hastily no doubt, as he had failed to notice the mismatched margins of the typewriter. He left by the front door, which as I had proved earlier could be done, though a few minutes of setup time were required. All in all, I figured the murder to have taken less than a half hour.

I took another sip of my drink, this time a small one, and closed my eyes. The next thing I wanted to do was to establish motive. I opened my eyes and jotted Richard's name down on the left-hand side of an empty page of my sketchbook. Halfway down I did the same with Sir Colin. On the right, beside each of these names, I wrote the names Hara, Keller, Clissac, Borromini, Piruzzi and Cavalliere. At the bottom of the page I wrote "Elena Piruzzi? Servants?" I stared at the list. Unless I was badly mistaken, among this group was the killer.

I started with Richard. Who had a motive for murdering him? Hara? I'd have to admit that I didn't think Hara capable of squashing a spider, but I know that the least suspected is often the most guilty, so Hara would have to be included. Did he have a motive? "Had gone to school with Richard in New Haven," I wrote. Seemed a bit envious, or perhaps *vengeful* was a better word, over the fact that Richard had garnered all of the recognition while they were schoolmates.

Then there was Keller. Though Keller hardly seemed capable of committing murder, he was certainly the most likely, I suspected, to do something, anything, to win the competition. He faced impending financial ruin which could have prompted him to action. And he had already tried to blackmail me, so there was little doubt, as he had told me, that he would do "whatever it takes" to win.

Clissac was next, and she had had something going with Richard, but I didn't quite know what. Of anyone at the villa, she was intense enough, it seemed to me, to kill. She had argued once or twice with Richard, but nothing serious as far as outward appearances would suggest.

Borromini was next. There was certainly no love lost between the two of them, and he had argued with Richard in the library before Richard's death. Sir Colin stated that they were at it the rest of the night, but not having been there for the whole episode I wasn't sure how it had ended. In any event, Borromini was a suspect.

Then there was Cavalliere. He hardly knew Richard and I couldn't think of anything between them, but it *was* significant that he was the one to find the body. He said that he saw Richard from his room in the villa and had gone to help him. I wondered if he was telling the truth, given that we had but his own word to go on.

And finally there was Piruzzi, who, as I had learned, was a shrewd and unpredictable personality. What was his real motive in inviting us all here? Did he have an ulterior motive that would lead him to set up a game of murder? He had been with Richard and Garbutt until shortly before they departed, and because of this he would have known the state Richard was in. He also had access to the wine cellar, which was possibly the source of the second bottle of wine. He could have done it, to be sure, but logic told me he wouldn't risk murder on the grounds of his own villa.

I then shifted my attention to the death of Sir Colin. Though his killing seemed to be linked to Richard's by virtue of the seven sacraments theme, I wondered if that had been intentional. Was there something Garbutt knew about Richard's murder, or about the state Richard was in at the time of his death, that led Richard's killer to kill him too? The importance of that couldn't be overstated, because it would nullify any other motive I could think of. On the other hand, if Garbutt was killed for another reason, what was it? I looked at my list again. Nothing jumped out at me except that Clissac had certainly feuded with Sir Colin, and again Cavalliere was the first at the scene of the crime. Was it possible that Cavalliere killed Garbutt in the time that he was sent to fetch him for dinner? If so, he would've been extremely efficient with his time, and he also then put on a credible acting job as I showed him how the killer locked the door from the inside. And besides, what possible reason could he have for the murders, unless as Piruzzi's loyal servant, he was acting on his behalf?

No, I was beginning to think that of all the motives I could establish, the strongest, and the one that could stir any of the architects into action, was the thought of reaping the rewards of Piruzzi's competition. That ruled out Cavalliere and Piruzzi. But it left three men and a woman who were competing for a prize that would set them up so that they would never have to work again. In the case of Keller, it would stave off disaster. The fewer the competitors, the higher one's chances of succeeding. The number was down to four, and if the two deaths could be chalked up to accident and suicide, then the killer, were he or she one of the architects, might hope the competition to continue. This was rational in the most pathological way, and I had to wonder what would happen next. The murderer couldn't expect to go on killing without repercussions, yet so far, the aspirations of the architects themselves had not deterred them from continuing to work. It would be interesting to see what would happen in the morning.

I set down my pad and rubbed my aching eyes. My mind was stimulated, but I was also aware of the fact that I hadn't slept in almost twenty-four hours. There was so much I wanted to know, and so much that still didn't make sense. I had to prepare my best case for Anghini, but I found myself unable to hold onto a thought. I turned out the light and drifted off to sleep, my mind turning like a big wheel, unbalanced and somewhat out of kilter. As I was slipping out of consciousness a face entered my thoughts. That of Elena Piruzzi. Intriguing Elena Piruzzi. I had to know more about her.

NINE

I wasn't sure if I was dreaming when I heard a faint sound from beneath my window. I slipped back into the dark unconscious, then heard it again, this time knowing it to be real. It was footfall noise and it seemed to be moving away. I eased out of the sheets and went to the front window. My head was still somewhat numb from vodka, and it took my eyes a moment to focus upon the scene below.

Someone was walking along the edge of the garden on a bee line for the main house. It was too dark to tell who it was, but the figure moved with purpose, and my eyes followed it until it neared the dining terrace. Suddenly I noticed another person beneath the terrace light, a man I thought, in a long coat with his hands deep in his pockets. He wore a wide-brimmed hat that hid his face, and as the first figure approached, he nodded, and the two of them disappeared into the night. It was then that I realized that the first figure was Pet Clissac.

I checked my watch. It was a quarter to four. I yanked on my trousers and went outside. It was cold now, and as I jogged across the garden my breath condensed in the chilly night air. My gait was stilted, my body like an automobile not quite warmed up, and I found myself wishing I were in better shape. I climbed the garden steps and rounded the house, emerging into the villa's forecourt. I saw nothing, so I continued on to the main gates and left the villa grounds.

The moon had moved across the broad black sky, and it now hung like a lantern over the serrated silhouette of a forest, the forest lying on either side of the road. I set off down the road, and in the distance I once again caught a glimpse of Clissac and the mystery man.

Who was he, I wondered. I thought back to my idea that Sir Colin's killer might have had an accomplice, and to my thoughts that Clissac was an intense-enough competitor to kill. Pet wasn't nearly large enough to have lifted Sir Colin to the ceiling, but with the help of someone else, she could have done it. I also recalled Piruzzi's warning the competitors not to leave the grounds of the villa. Clissac was skating on thin ice, not only risking expulsion from the competition but possibly having risked murder.

I followed them silently as the road began its steep descent down towards the lake. We were soon through the forest, and the road turned tightly along the face of the mountain, hugging the steep jagged sheets of stone. The direction of the asphalt kept changing, jerking abruptly at the end of each short stretch of grade. The hairpin turns kept me alert, even though I had been in bed not five minutes before.

I kept my distance as we wound down the mountain, and the two of them moved in silent haste, as if there were an urgency to their mission. Once or twice I nearly stumbled on the dark pavement, and I found it hard to both watch them and keep my eye on the road. We must have traveled the better part of a mile when, at a certain point, I was paying attention to the road and lost them. I rounded a bend and peered ahead of me into the darkness, but they were gone. I stopped abruptly. My heart was pounding. The skin on my skull felt as though it had been shrink-wrapped.

My eyes searched the ground around me. I was on a steep rugged portion of the road. It was too steep for them to have left the asphalt, and there was nothing in the way of cover in which they could hide. I started walking again, pondering the situation. I broke into a trot and soon came upon a side road, no more than a cart path, that veered off to my right.

Without pausing I took the cart path and soon, up ahead, the outline of a small domed building rose out of a line of dark trees. We had moved around the side of the mountain and were in a small crook between Piruzzi's mountain and another. I saw them again, much closer than before, and I realized that their pace was slowing. I paused and watched as they continued on up towards the building. The building was a small village church. I could see a few houses surrounding the church, nestled in between the hills. In the split second I shifted my attention to them, Clissac and her companion once again disappeared.

I walked cautiously from that point on, soon coming upon a high stone wall. It was old and crumbling, and I walked along its base, finally arriving at an iron gate, the only opening in the wall. I halted.

Through the gate and enclosed by the wall was a small well-ordered cemetery. It was organized along a straight path, and on either side of the path were ancient ossuaries, each made of fragmented white marble slabs that glowed beneath the moonlight. It was quiet in the cemetery, no sign of human life. The scent of cedar hung heavily in the dark damp air. I tugged at the gate handle, but it didn't budge.

The stone wall connected to the church just fifty feet beyond the gate. Unable to get the gate open, I walked softly up to the front porch of the church, where two deeply worn marble steps took me to the door. The door was old and long since painted, its surface scarred by the ravages of time. It was perhaps ten feet high and carved long ago with ornate patterns that I could hardly see but that were evident to the touch. I found an oversized knob and pulled. The door opened silently and I stood at the entrance, not sure whether I wanted to go in. I had come this far, though, so I couldn't stop now.

I stepped across the threshold and into the nave, and gently pulled the door to behind me. There was very little light inside, and I hesitated while my eyes adjusted to the blackness. There was a musty odor in the calm air and the faintest hint of incense. Water dripped from somewhere beyond the nave, but other than that, not a sound was to be heard.

I started forward down the aisle of the church, and at each careful step the sound of my leather soles echoed in the emptiness of the space. Where were they, I wondered. I wanted to know what they were doing here, but I didn't want them to know that I had followed. There was no sign of life—no lights, no human activity—and I couldn't imagine what had brought them to this lonely place. But they had to be here, and I decided that I would wait in silence. I stepped to my left and slipped into a pew, resting my exhausted bones.

Water continued dripping, and the wind picked up, rattling old windows that lined the side aisles of the church like a choir of ghosts crying out from the dead. The longer I sat, the more I could sense the space, not with my eyes so much as with my other faculties, an almost hyperreal state in which my body situated itself into the being of the place. An owl hooted in the distance. The coolness of the pew absorbed its way into my back. A floorboard creaked beneath my feet. Stilted dust rolled across my nose.

I thought I heard voices once, but they evaporated into the darkness. A light that appeared from beyond the altar existed ultimately only in my imagination. I was growing more tired with each tick of my watch and my breathing slowed to nothing. My head started bobbing. I couldn't hold my eyes open. I lapsed into sleep.

TEN

I awoke with a start and found myself staring into the sagging eyes of an old woman who was hunched over a dustpan, her face not ten feet from my own. She wore a heavy woolen skirt fronted by a dirty apron. In her hands she held a handmade straw broom with a bright scarlet handle, the color matched by the patterned kerchief that was wrapped tightly around her head. Her pale eyes were capped by thick dark eyebrows, manly eyebrows, and her ancient pockmarked face held stray hairs. She was in the center aisle of the little church, and I was still in a pew. My muscles were sore, my neck stiff, and my mouth welded shut by dried saliva.

The sun was up, and dust swirled in the warm shafts of light that streamed through the encrusted side-aisle windows, simple windows in a simple church that probably no longer had a reason for being in this hamlet. What I hadn't been able to see in the darkness of the night before was the church's state of disrepair—cracked walls in need of paint and plaster, fixtures in need of replacement, a leaky roof. Everything had a dinginess to it, but ignoring the church's condition, the old woman cleaned, in a hopeless battle against its ultimate decay.

I waited for an opportune moment, until her eyes had left me, then I rose and attempted to smooth out my clothes before walking stiffly towards the front door. I left a small contribution in the candle box and stepped out into the warm morning sun. My watch said that it was half past nine, and I figured I had already missed breakfast at the villa. I started back up the cart path, the sun over my shoulder, the lake shimmering in all its glory. I was upset with myself for having fallen asleep, and even more so for having failed to see Clissac and her companion. I wondered if I should confront her, or at least tell Piruzzi, but the closer I got to the main gates of the villa, the more I thought I would use the knowledge to my advantage, hoping at some other time to return to the church and see if I could find out what had drawn them there.

I soon reached the villa, and as I entered the house, the uniformed servants were hurrying across the main hall, piles of empty dishes balanced on their arms, confirming for me that I had just missed the morning meal. I reached the dining terrace and found an all but empty table there. I then saw Piruzzi beyond the terrace, strolling in the garden with his dog, leisurely enjoying the brilliant day. The dog, a scruffy liver-and-white English springer spaniel, had more energy than I considered possible at this hour of the morning. As I approached, it leapt at my legs.

"Down boy," Piruzzi said. "Jamie, good morning. I was beginning to worry about you." I found the statement disturbing, given that it was qualified by the word *beginning*. Had no one thought it odd that I hadn't shown for breakfast?

I decided to let it pass.

"I went for a walk," I said.

He looked me up and down and winced slightly at the state of my clothes.

"You should have some breakfast," he said. "I'll have the staff put together a little something."

"That can wait," I said, reaching down to pet the dog. "Can you and I go phone Anghini? I want to talk with him about what we discussed. And about something else I discovered."

He stroked his moustache, which at this hour, at least, was in bushy disarray. The whites of his eyes were pinkish, and he looked as though he needed some sleep.

"That would be the lock on Garbutt's door," he said.

"Yes, yes. Franco told me about it. Very clever of you to figure it out."

"I think it proves I'm not imagining things. Could we give Anghini a call?"

"I've already talked with him," Piruzzi said. "I filled him in on it all. The other wine, the seven sacraments, the lock."

"What'd he say?" I asked.

"He was impressed. He said that he would look into it. I expect he'll come around this afternoon. He's waiting on Garbutt's autopsy report."

I felt a wave of relief. I couldn't help but break into a smile.

"What happens in the meantime?" I asked. "Will you cancel the competition?"

"I discussed that with Anghini, too. He told me he'd like us to continue, if for no other reason than to keep the competitors in Salò until the investigation is wound up."

"Do you think it'll work? Won't they be too scared?"

"As far as they know, Garbutt committed suicide. I brought up canceling the competition with them at breakfast. We took a vote, and the others voted three to one to go on. Only Borromini voted against continuing."

Typical. I thought back to Elena's description of the architects as a greedy lot. On the other hand, their decision to give in to greed didn't factor in the fact that murder was involved. Would they have voted to go on if they'd known?

"Don't you think," I said, "that we should tell them the truth?"

"If we do," said Piruzzi, "and they vote to discontinue, then the group will be gone. Anghini desires enough time to finish Garbutt's autopsy."

"So we'll do as we're told, huh?"

"With one exception, I hope."

"What's that?" I asked.

"We will of course keep Anghini apprised of any new developments, but . . ."

"But what?"

"Well . . . so far, you've been able to figure out far more than the police."

"Agreed."

"I don't know how to say this."

"Say it, please."

"It's . . . ah . . . Do you think you could report everything to me *before* we talk with the inspector?"

"You're worried about publicity," I said.

"Yes. And about my responsibility to my guests. I think that as you are advising me on the competition, you might also advise me in the matter of these deaths. I'll give you free reign. And . . . if you like, I could pay you an additional sum."

"No compensation needed," I said. "I'm being paid too much as it is. I'll do what I can."

He smiled. "I knew you would."

The spaniel started tugging at its lead.

"Then I'll have the staff prepare you some breakfast," he said.

"Thank you."

"Oh, and Jamie," he said as his dog pulled him away, "I also expect an update on the competition. Tonight, at dinner, yes?"

I nodded and watched him stride away.

I spent the better part of the rest of the day checking on the architects, not just with regard to the competition, but also trying to ferret out what I could that might shift suspicion to any one of them. As my curiosity was high regarding Clissac's nocturnal wanderings, I started with her first.

"Jamie, my dear, come in," she said, greeting me at her door. She showed no signs of having been up most of the night, and she invited me right up to her studio. The first thing I noticed was her typewriter, the same model as Sir Colin's.

"How's it going?" I asked.

"Good," she said. She grabbed me by the hand and led me to her drafting table. By now, twenty-four hours after having begun the competition, she had generated more sketches and thrown away more wads of paper than I would have thought humanly possible. Somewhere within the mounds were a few select sheets, color pencil sketches on yellow bumwad, along with a tiny basswood model.

"What do you think?" she asked.

I stared down at the pile of sketches and began thumbing my way through them. They were decorated with graphite smudges and coffee stains, but all in all skillfully delineated. I picked up the model and rotated it in my hand. It was no bigger than a makeup compact, though built with jewelry-like precision. The building design was essentially the same as that which I had seen before, severe Deconstructivism. But into that fray she had now added a number of human sculptural forms, tiny writhing figures that hung about the structural elements of her building like flies on flypaper. They really didn't go with her design, and I wondered if they were simply an attempt to appease Piruzzi, whose taste was known to run somewhere to the conservative side of Clissac's convoluted expressionism.

"Well, provocative," was all I could come up with.

She pulled a cigarette from a silver case and started to light it. She paused, and instead she rubbed out the lit match on her drawing table with her bare thumb.

"You don't like it," she said, visibly upset, balancing the unlit brown cigarette between her lips. She pulled her parallel edge down on the drawing board so I could get a better look at the drawings.

"I didn't say that," I replied. "I guess I don't understand it."

She sighed. I recognized the reaction. I was supposed to get sucked into a debate with her. Her professional life revolved around theory, and discourse was the method by which she exerted her beliefs. I didn't have the energy to pursue it.

"What's this here?" I asked, changing the topic and referring to a small cubicle she had drawn in the middle of her chapel plan. "A confessional?"

"No," she said, laughing. "It's hardly the size of a phone booth. Just big enough for one, God knows not two. And I don't believe in confession anyway."

"But Renzo's program required that a confessional be provided for the chapel."

"He'll not get it from me," she said.

"Then what is it?"

"An eschatological reflection chamber."

"A what?"

"A booth for reflecting on the end . . . the end of one's life."

"Quaint," I said. "And how long does one have to stay in this booth?"

"As long as it takes . . . to come to terms with death."

Death and confession, I thought. Rather topical subjects of late.

"Did you work on the chapel all night?" I asked.

She looked at me suspiciously. For a moment I thought that she might know something, that she had seen me following her.

"Certainly not," she said. "My design will be finished when it's finished. On my terms. On my own schedule. Piruzzi's offer of millions and that manuscript will not affect me. I'll not produce a spurious design just to reap his rewards."

"Well, the drawings are due at breakfast, you know."

"I know," she said smugly.

She finally lit her cigarette, and she spent the next few minutes in deep thought among her clouds of gray vapor.

I could tell she was done with me, and I slipped out the door.

I next went to Thornburgh Keller's pavilion, and he answered almost immediately after I knocked. His sleeves were rolled up and shirt untucked, and at least from the look of his studio, he seemed to be working at a frenetic pace. But perhaps it was too busy a pace, or a simple lack of focus, because the products of his labor were common. I've seen better work from my first-year graduate students, and it's doubtful that any one of them will ever reach Keller's stature in the profession.

His design for the chapel could only be described as a lapse into the Modern classicism that he'd practiced in the 1960s—scaleless, brutal, badly proportioned, and stripped bare of even the most subtle hint of talent. I think that even he knew the work to be inferior, because he kept shifting the conversation away from the competition and towards other subjects, even though he knew that in less than twenty-four hours, his drawings would be judged by Piruzzi.

I did confirm while I was there that his drawing table was equipped with a parallel edge, and that the wire was still intact and in service. I also confirmed that he had a typewriter like Sir Colin's. At a certain point during my time there, he excused himself to use the bathroom. I took the opportunity to type a few sample lines onto a piece of scrap paper from the machine.

From Keller's pavilion I made my way back to my own, where again I had lunch in my rooms. After lunch I went to see Hara, who by this point in the competition, was in full stride. His model was essentially finished, a work of art unto itself, matched only by the hauntingly beautiful charcoal sketches that hung on the walls of his studio.

His chapel was unusual, but without the aggressiveness of Pet Clissac's design. It had an aesthetic that an architect could admire, and yet it would not be too avant-garde for the lay person. It was coolly modern, made of cast-in-place concrete with teak windows, infill partitions of stainless steel and maple. The interior of the chapel had large maneuverable walls of maple paneling, hung from the ceiling like theater flies. The walls could be dropped to the floor of the chapel in a number of ingenious geometric configurations, giving the chapel the possibility of multiple floor plans depending on its use, the time of year (as related to the sun path), and so forth. The roof of the chapel was the most extraordinary feature of all, a complex amalgam of Bezier curves punctuated with deep skylights to filter light down into the space below.

"I suppose you're almost finished," I said, after having examined the impressive work.

"Yes," he said. He seemed a bit stiff, like something was bothering him.

"Anything the matter?" I asked.

"I don't like what's happening," he said. "The fact that there's death about."

He straightened the collar of his olive green linen shirt, then walked over to his model. It was almost done, but he seemed to be touching up the final complex planes that made up the roof. I considered what I knew about the deaths of Richard and Sir Colin, and I fought off the temptation to somehow give him a warning.

He turned to me and spoke softly.

"I believe someone was in here today," he said nervously.

"How do you know?"

"I can just sense it. A different smell maybe, or something out of place. I can't quite say. My first worry was that someone had tried to sabotage my drawings."

"Well, did they?"

"No. Nothing's been disturbed."

"You should keep your door locked," I said. "You only have a few more hours before you present to Piruzzi."

"Believe me, I will," he said.

He went back to work on the model. Though he seemed genuinely upset at the fact that his pavilion had been violated, I couldn't be sure he was telling the truth. I took the opportunity to wander around the studio, pretending to look at his drawings, but also searching for his typewriter. I found it on a table in the corner of the room, along with his reference books. It was the same model typewriter as Sir Colin's. He also had a parallel edge, set up on his drafting board with the wire intact. I checked his kitchenette for wine, but there was none. In fact, he had nothing alcoholic whatsoever.

I then excused myself and walked across the garden to Borromini's pavilion. He called for me to enter, and as I stepped into the upstairs studio, I found him hard at work on an analytique, a type of watercolor rendering of a building that combines a partial plan with a section, along with elevation details. They are generally done of classical buildings, in muted colors, with shade and shadow realistically conveyed, and the whole composition set within a decorative border. Borromini was presently using a thin dry brush, applying *faux marbre* to an elevation detail of an elaborate Corinthian column.

"Jamie," he said, "how are you?"

He held the brush with remarkable steadiness, and his torso, even extended over the easel, remained perfectly still. His body showed no sign of fatigue, but his eyes had dark rings under them, and his furrowed brow denoted that the analytique was a strain on his eyes.

"Fine," I said. "But the greater question is, how are you?"

"Oh, I'll make it. Not long now."

I looked around the rest of the studio. The drawings he had done earlier on parchment were still there, lying neatly under his old T-square. On a table behind his drawing board was a small model made of plaster of Paris. It was a sketch model really, made to give some idea of the massing of his chapel design. Detail would be communicated by the analytique.

"It's looking good, Gio," I said. "Are you submitting any written description with your drawings? You know, to give Piruzzi a better idea of materials?"

"I probably will," he said. "If I have time."

"I just noticed that you don't have a typewriter."

"No, I had Cavalliere remove it. Jamie, you know me well enough to know that, on principle, I wouldn't use a typewriter. I'll write some notes out longhand . . . if I get a chance."

I noticed his quill pen, still on the drafting table.

"Is there anything you need from me?" I asked.

"How are you at watercolor?" He grinned and tipped the brush in my direction.

"Looks to me as if you're doing fine. Plus, you wouldn't cheat would you?" I asked jokingly. "I'd be loath to help . . . unless you agree to split the prize with me. If you win, that is."

"What do want? The Vitruvius or the five million?"

I pretended to be in deep thought.

"I'll take either, or *half* of each."

He held his laughter for a brief second, before it burst.

Back in my pavilion I recorded all I had learned about the competition in my notebook, and then what little I had learned about the murders in my sketchbook. By six o'clock I felt no closer to discovering who the murderer was than I had the night before. Finally, after reviewing my notes again, I remembered that I wanted to check the wine cellar.

I made my way to the main house and to the kitchen deep within it. It was a world of scrubbed white tile and brushed stainless steel, bright hammered copper and oaken butcher block. The kitchen was inflated with the strong sweet aroma of northern Italian cuisine and three decidedly jovial male cooks, who were, upon my entrance, harmonizing (at least trying to) the final parts of "Nessun dorma" in an *appassionato ad libitum* mode. Pavarotti, Domingo, and Carreras they were not.

"I'm looking for Franco Cavalliere," I said to an older gentleman, who worked at the stove between his two assistants and whose voice had dominated the aria.

"He's gone to town," he said. "Can I be of assistance? I'm Liserio—Paolo Liserio."

As he spoke, he stood over a simmering saucepan, stirring it with the precise movement of an orchestra conductor, making strong deliberate figure eights with a wooden spoon. He was a thin man of average height, though his stomach was well rounded, no doubt due to his profession. His gay rosy face was set off by a wild nest of wispy white hair, and his mouth had an empty look to it, as if he were missing some teeth.

"Franco told me he would give me a tour of the wine cellar. I'm a bit of an oenophile, I'm afraid."

This was a lie, but I figured if Cavalliere was somehow tied up with the murders, then he might try to hide evidence. I preferred that someone else show me the cellar.

"I would be happy to show it to you."

"That would be nice, but you're busy . . ."

"No, no, no. This I leave to my assistants. It's time they earned their keep."

He handed the spoon to one of his assistants and gave him a few instructions in rapid Italian. He then motioned me out, by way of a back door, and I followed him through the pantry, where another door led us to a service stairwell. As we descended, the air became cooler, and soon we came upon a subterranean passage of heavy stone. It was a constricted corridor, vaulted overhead, dimly lit by dust-infested bare bulbs that were screwed into aged porcelain sockets. We wound our way past any number of heavy wooden doors and soon came upon a broad doorway at the end of the passage. Liserio pulled a large set of keys from his pocket and unlocked the door. As he opened it, we were greeted by the sweet moldy odor of the cellar itself, and we stepped inside.

The room temperature was the first thing that I noticed. I saw no sign of refrigeration equipment, but it was

cool, cooler than the corridor and just the right environment for wine. We were no doubt at the north end of the
villa. The room was long and low and covered by shallow
stone pendentive vaults. The vaults in turn came down
upon heavy piers, and between the piers, there were tall
wooden racks that held countless bottles of wine. There
must have been several thousand dusty bottles, so many
in fact that I could hardly see the walls. The wooden
racks formed a Cartesian grid, each square marked by a
small yellow or red dot that denoted the lead cork cap at
the top of a bottle of wine. In a far corner, several barrels
of wine stood upon wooden cradles, and next to these
barrels any number of jeroboams and methuselahs, the
leviathans of the wine world, occupied larger racks. I love
wine, and God knows I drink my share of it. I can't
profess to be a true connoisseur, but I do know a great
collection when I see one. And I was seeing one now.

"Phenomenal," I said.

I ran my fingers over the embossed insignias of wines
whose names I knew only from wine books, too valuable,
I imagined, to actually exist in real life.

"Thank you," Liserio replied with a certain undeni-
able pride. His assured smile told me that he had a hand
in amassing this tour de force.

I walked slowly around the room. At each section I
stopped and pulled bottles from the racks. Vietto Barolo
'71. Château Y'Quem '64. A '49 Borgogno Barolo. The
collection was composed mostly of the best Italian wines,
with some classified French growth thrown in for good
measure.

I then stopped admiring long enough to remember my
purpose in being here. I recalled the scent of the wine in
the glass next to Richard's body, a powerful tannic
aroma. I was hoping it had come from the cellar. My first
thought, having now seen the cellar, was that it had been
a red Bordeaux. My own most profound memories of
tannic powerhouses were the occasions in my life when I
had been treated to, or had spent my last penny on, a

superb first-or second-growth Bordeaux. But upon re-examining the Bordeaux bins before me, I realized that they were full. Unless a bottle had been taken and the supply later replenished, it couldn't have come from this collection.

"Doesn't Renzo drink his Bordeaux?" I asked.

Liserio smiled and joined me at the bin. "No. For the *dottore,* it's an investment. He saves them mostly, in order to trade for his real love . . . the Italian reds."

I pulled a bottle from the rack. It was a Château Mouton-Rothschild '45, worth at least several thousand dollars. No doubt valuable as trade bait.

If he didn't drink his French wine then, it meant that if the second bottle had come from the cellar, then it came from one of the racks of Italian reds. I combed the surrounding bins. There were thousands of bottles in these racks, but there were also many bottles missing. To find the right one would be impossible.

"Do you keep an inventory?" I asked hopefully.

"We do."

He stepped back out into the hall, where from a wall hook next to the door he pulled a clipboard. Its pages were full of writing.

"Do you mind if I have a look?"

He gave me an inquisitive glance but handed me the clipboard.

The top of the first sheet listed days of the week in Italian, and below each was a place to write in inventory. How many bottles of a particular type that came in or out were listed, and on what day the transaction had occurred. At the bottom was a total for each day, and far to the right-hand side a place for the initials of the person who had made a particular transaction. Last night, for instance, "FC," meaning Franco Cavalliere I supposed, had taken out four bottles of Valpolicella Classico Girardi and two bottles of Recioto Masi. This would have been the wine we had with dinner.

There was a similar record for the day before. Except

for one thing. "FC" had also taken out a single bottle of Chianti Antinori. On the day that Richard died. I couldn't believe my eyes.

"This log is fairly accurate?" I asked.

Liserio said: "Once a week the racks are checked against the log. A bottle cannot leave the shelf without being recorded in the book. We had an incident a few years back where one of the servants was stealing. This can no longer happen."

"Who checks the log?" I asked.

"I do."

"And what day of the week do you check?"

"Saturday. You can see my initials there at the bottom, next to the weekly total."

"So you knew about this bottle?" I asked referring to the Chianti Antinori.

He stared at the log, then shook his head.

"No. That wasn't there on Saturday. It shouldn't be there. You can see, it doesn't total up with the numbers at the bottom."

"Whose initials are *FC?*" I asked.

He looked up at me. "Franco Cavalliere's," he said.

"Do you know any reason he would have taken that wine and not logged it in until later?"

"As for taking the wine, Franco is free to do as he pleases. He has a key to the cellar. As for why he didn't log it in until later, I can't say. He must have forgotten to log it, then remembered after I had done my weekly check."

Had he, I wondered. I had to stop and think. I found it hard to believe that if Cavalliere were the killer, he would've been so careless as to take a bottle from the cellar knowing that there was a log, or even more, if he had, that he would've recorded it in the book. It must be a coincidence. I wondered how I could find out without confronting him.

"Who else has the key to the cellar?" I asked.

"Myself . . . the *dottore* . . . Cavalliere . . . and Elena."

"Will you do me a favor?" I said. "Ask Franco why he didn't log out that wine."

"Why?"

I didn't have a lie that sounded plausible.

"I'm afraid I can't tell you," I said. "But if you like, talk to the *dottore* about it. I'm sure he would want you to do as I say."

He tilted his head slightly and nodded. "As you wish," he said.

"Well, I should let you get back upstairs. Thank you so much for the tour."

A few minutes later I entered the library, where a thin little woman in a maid's uniform was busy dusting bookshelves with a feather duster that seemed at least half her size. Her wrists were her only body parts that actually moved, until, as I watched with furtive interest, she shuffled forward in big black shoes, the kind of heavy footwear that it seemed was not made to leave the terra firma. Her hair was an unnatural red, and gray roots showed through like garden weeds into an otherwise perfect lawn. She looked at me with the sort of long rude look that usually isn't rude at all, but rather a sign of poor eyesight. I smiled and made my way to the bar.

I mixed myself a vodka martini, dropped in a plump olive, took a sip and soaked in my surroundings.

The bar was carefully appointed. Expensive bottles of liquor jockeyed for space with the wine cellar's finest. Several of the *dottore*'s robust reds were standing upright in a glass cruvinet cabinet that rested upon a thick verde antique marble countertop. To the right of the cabinet, pieces of Christofle silver were lined up like soldiers ready for service, though their flawless arrangement seemed to dare anyone to use them. Below the bar, several stainless steel undercounter refrigerators were stocked to the gills with stout German and eastern European lagers and pilsners. Above the bar Murano glassware stood upon sheer Venetian lace, the lace fitting glove-like onto a number of tiered walnut shelves. The shelves were backed up by beveled glass mirrors, and the reflections of the glassware created a fractured ambiguity not unlike in Édouard Manet's painting *The Bar at the Folies-Bergère*.

Also on these shelves was a collection of crystal wine-glasses, including some tulip-shaped ones, similar in design to the one found next to Richard's body. I picked one up and rolled its fine stem between my fingers.

"Mi scusi," I called to the maid, who had by now made her way to the opposite side of the room. "Do you clean this room every day?" I asked in Italian.

Her feather duster froze.

"Yes sir," she responded. "I clean all the ground floor rooms. Each and every day. The sun comes up, I clean. The sun sets, I go home."

"Yesterday, did you notice anything unusual about the bar here?"

She walked slowly in my direction and stared up at me with squinting eyes.

"No sir."

"By chance were there any wineglasses missing?"

"I wouldn't know. I only clean and straighten the bar. The kitchen staff cleans the glasses. It's not my job."

"Were there any empty wine bottles on the bar here yesterday?"

I was thinking of the empty Chianti from the wine cellar log, though I didn't really expect it to have shown up here after the murder.

"No."

"Figures," I said to myself. "A shot in the dark."

"What's that, sir?"

"Nothing. Look, if you do remember that anything was missing, or anything out of the ordinary, please let the *dottore* or me know."

"I'm afraid I've never spoken to the *dottore,"* she said. "But I'll tell Signor Cavalliere, if you wish."

"No! I mean that's not necessary. No need to bother him. Just tell me if you think of anything."

She paused as if she was befuddled, then nodded politely. She then started across the room before turning and, again with a long stare, saying: "By the way. Who are you?"

"Jamie Ramsgill. I'm working for the *dottore.*"

She shuffled across the room to her dusting, and I went back to my drink. I sipped slowly, thinking some more about the state of the bar. I then started for the dining terrace, where I thought I could sit and try to pull all that I knew together. Piruzzi would want his report after dinner.

"Signor Ramsgill," she said somewhat surprisingly, before I could exit the room. "There *was* something missing. I just remembered. A corkscrew."

My mind replayed the scenario for Richard's death. The murderer choked Richard to death, then decided he needed another bottle. I didn't know where the second bottle had come from, but of course he had to get it open. He must have come to the library and taken a corkscrew. I felt as though the proverbial light bulb had just gone on over my head.

"Where was it?" I asked.

"It would have been out on the bar that evening. Signor Cavalliere serves wine to the guests after dinner. He normally returns it to the top left drawer when he's finished. When I cleaned up yesterday, it wasn't there."

"Did you say something to him?" I asked.

"To Signor Cavalliere? Oh, no sir."

I walked to the drawers left of the refrigerators and opened the top one. A silver-plated corkscrew with the initials "RPP" engraved upon it stared me in the face, the overhead wall washer lights glimmering against its polished surface.

"So you replaced it with a new one?" I asked.

"No sir." She moved towards me and looked into the drawer.

"No. That's it. Someone returned it."

"Are you sure?"

"Yes sir. That's the corkscrew. You see, it has the *dottore*'s initials on it. And it wasn't in the drawer yesterday."

I considered her statement that Franco usually placed it in the drawer at the end of the evening. That would be routine, as the *dottore* entertained regularly, and as far as I knew the other servants were allowed to go home after dinner. Franco was the only staff member who lived at the villa, and therefore he performed after-dinner duties. Why hadn't he returned the corkscrew to the drawer the night Richard died, as was his custom? Had he used it for a different purpose? Had he forgotten it until later? I could think of but one purpose and it sent a chill up my spine. It was possible that someone else had taken it, but how would they have known to return it to that particular drawer? And Cavalliere had taken a bottle of Chianti from the cellar, which fit the bill as the tannic wine I had sniffed in the glass next to Richard's body. That was two incriminating strikes against him.

I thought back to the motives I had established for each of the suspects. Cavalliere didn't have one, or at least not one that I'd uncovered. But he did have opportunity. Better opportunity than anyone. Except for his own accounts of what had happened just prior to finding the two dead bodies, he could have easily killed them both. *Finally,* I thought. I'm getting somewhere.

I thanked the maid for her assistance and stepped out onto the dining terrace, pondering my next move. I should discuss what I knew with Piruzzi, though I somehow felt I hadn't done enough to eliminate the others as suspects. If I told what I knew at this point, I might embarrass myself, or worse yet, put myself in danger. I needed the freedom to talk to the others, and Piruzzi had to let them know that there was the suspicion of murder. If he truly wanted a full accounting of what had happened, then each fact had to be brought to the surface.

It was just at that very moment that I saw Elena

Piruzzi. She was strolling up from the woods with her video camera in hand, the sun caressing her long dark hair. She wore loose khaki work clothes that contradicted her supple frame. As she made her way over to the dining terrace, she smiled.

"That looks good," she said, eyeing my martini. "May I join you?"

I offered to get her a drink. She accepted and I returned from the library a moment later with the Cinzano and soda she had requested. She took the cool glass and pressed it to her tanned forehead. I could smell her perfume, a subtle aroma like that of a fading daffodil.

"Reward for a hard day's work," she said.

She closed her eyes and tilted her head until the low yellow sun struck her smooth chin. The collar of her shirt was damp around the neck, but she appeared so perfect to me that I hardly thought it possible she could perspire.

She said unexpectedly: "I've heard from Cavalliere that you believe the two architects were murdered."

Her words caught me by surprise.

"Yes."

"Cavalliere says you've discovered some rather interesting connections. What do the police say about what you've found?"

"I haven't spoken to them. Your father has."

She leaned back in the chair and gently swung her hair over her shoulder.

"I see," she said. "And he's asked you to let him handle all relations with the police. Am I right?"

"How'd you know?"

"Father's very good at avoiding the wrong type of publicity."

I took a sip of my martini.

"And he wouldn't let something like two minor murders upset his competition," she continued.

I put down my glass and leaned forward.

"It was the police who asked to have the competition

continue," I said. "They asked for it in order to keep the other architects here in Salò."

"Father told you this?"

"Yeah."

"And you believed him?"

"What do you mean?"

"Well, as I told you before, Mr. Ramsgill, Father almost always gets his way. My guess is that he convinced the police to allow him to continue."

"Why?"

"So he can continue his onslaught of a natural habitat."

"You're still upset about the chapel?"

"Of course. Wouldn't you be, if you were me?"

I had been pondering our earlier conversation. I wondered to what lengths she would go to stop the *dottore*'s chapel from being built. I also wondered how she was taking the fact that a significant chunk of her inheritance would be going to one of the architects.

"Can I ask you a question?"

"You just did," she said.

"No, seriously. Please don't take this the wrong way, but could I ask where you were when the two men died?"

She looked at me askance.

"Why?"

"Just curious."

She drained the better part of her drink from the glass.

"Like everyone else," she said. "I was asleep when your friend died."

"And at the time of Sir Colin's death?"

She hesitated. "I was in the woods," she said. "I'm there every day until sunset."

"Is there anyone who can vouch for you?"

She laughed.

"My, my, Mr. Ramsgill. You must have all sorts of ideas in that appealing little head of yours."

"Call me Jamie. And you don't have to answer that if you don't want to."

"Oh, I don't care. No, I saw no one, at least not at the time he died. Though actually . . ."

"Actually what?"

"Finish your drink," she said. "I'll show you. And then maybe I'll be off the hook."

ELEVEN

On the north side of the villa, beyond a double row of arches, was a small courtyard. Its walls were bathed by the late afternoon sun, and they were formed by a continuous arched loggia, above which planes of orange stucco were dotted with tiny dark windows, the order of the whole not unlike a monastic cloister. The courtyard was anchored at the four corners by dense obelisk-like topiaries. At its center was a small oval pool. The pool contained enough water to make it look inviting, and the water was as still and reflective as a slab of polished black granite, which was in fact the material from which the pool had been constructed.

"You know," Elena said, unlocking a wide door in the shadows of the courtyard's eastern side, "it's not every day that I let a handsome man I hardly know into my boudoir."

My eyes caught her coy smile, just as it left her lips. I tried to gauge whether the smile was a come-on, or whether I was simply reading too much into it. There was a time when I would have known for sure, when, I suppose, my male instincts were sharper, undampened by years of failed half-hearted relationships, or intellectualized celibacy. I studied her face further, and her body, which curved in the most exquisite way. She exuded sensuality, from her soothing yellow eyes to her long satiny legs.

"I'm harmless," I said.

She nodded skeptically.

"You'd better be," she said jokingly. "Since there's a murderer on the loose."

She then opened the door and stepped aside, but only partially so, leaving just enough space between herself and the doorjamb for me to squeeze by. I smiled as I passed, catching the fragrance of perfume that rose from the open collar of her khaki shirt, just as my elbow brushed against her breast, which in the confines of the doorway, could not be avoided. She made no attempt to pull away, fully aware of the power she exerted over me. From the look in her eyes I could tell she was enjoying herself. She stepped away from the door, smiled, then motioned me forward.

We entered a suite of light-filled rooms, organized around a living area built upon a floor of terra-cotta tile. On one side of the space, French doors lead to a balcony, and on the other was a tall stone fireplace, above which, unless I was mistaken, was a polychrome ceramic cartouche by one of the Della Robbias. Several brass birdcages hung from the ceiling, and their inhabitants chirped excitedly as we entered the living area. I watched Elena as she systematically covered them up one by one with dark cloth.

"That'll quiet them," she said. "Have a seat."

I sat on a leather sofa that I recognized as one of Piruzzi S.p.A.'s most expensive pieces, as she stepped over to a painted armoire, rococo in design. She opened the armoire to reveal a television with a built-in videocassette recorder. Above the TV she found the tape she wanted, then she popped it into the tape machine. With the remote control in hand, she joined me on the sofa.

"My alibi," she said with a sly grin as she fast-forwarded the tape. She kicked off her shoes and revealed toes manicured to perfection. Her chin thrust forward, and I watched her as she watched jerky images speeding across the screen. She soon slowed the videotape to a normal speed, then looked back in my direction. She caught me staring at her. Just then the audio came back on.

"Now pay attention," she said. "This is yesterday. As you can see, I'm down in the woods."

The image was of raking light sifting through tall trees and filtering down to the forest floor. In the background, birds could be heard, as well as the faraway sounds of traffic around the lake. A voice-over accompanied the picture, Elena narrating at a whisper her observations of the birds.

"There," she said, stopping the tape. "That's family Alpha. My control group."

I couldn't see anything, but I took her word for it that the camera was now pointed at something in the way of birds at the top of the screen.

"From the time indicator there, you can see that it's seven o'clock."

She resumed the playback.

In the lower right-hand corner of the screen the date and time were digitally superimposed on the video image. I watched and listened for a few minutes until I had assured myself that indeed it was her talking, and that she was also holding the camera. I then realized something.

"Wait a minute," I said. "How do I know that you just didn't set the time and date to make it look like yesterday?"

"Oh, you are testy, aren't you?" she said.

She fast-forwarded again. We watched as images sped by. Suddenly the camera swung around and pointed up to the back of one of the pavilions. She slowed the tape to normal speed. The time indicator now read 8:18 P.M.

She said: "I heard some commotion just about here, and it frightened the birds."

I listened carefully and soon heard the sound of loud

knocking. I then heard a crash, and Piruzzi yelling Garbutt's name. The camera swept up to the second-story windows, and soon, I could see several of us behind the glass. We were looking out the back of Sir Colin's pavilion. At the time we broke in and found his body.

"Lord," I said in a whisper. Just to see it again was chilling, a kind of technological déjà vu.

Elena put her finger on the pause button and turned to me. Her eyes glistened softly as she spoke.

"Now do you believe me?" she asked.

I nodded.

"At first I was upset that someone had scared the birds away," she continued. "But then I realized that something must be amiss. When I later asked Father what had happened, he described the Englishman's suicide. It was Franco who told me of your murder suspicions."

I considered where that left me. If anything had changed.

"Could you rewind the tape?" I said.

She did so and I had her stop at a little after five o'clock, about the time I left Sir Colin's pavilion.

"You heard commotion at around eight," I said. "Did you hear anything earlier?"

I was wondering if she had heard anything when the murderer actually came to call on Sir Colin, sometime between when I left and 8:18.

"No," she said. "When I learned you suspected murder, I specifically went back through the tape comparing it to my field notes. To see if I had captured something. But I hadn't."

I took her word for it. For the first time, I felt that someone had been eliminated as a suspect. And, it seemed, I had an ally.

"Whom do you suspect?" she asked.

I eased back into the soft leather of the sofa and looked around the room. It was ridiculous, but somehow I wondered if we were being watched.

"Cavalliere," I said softly. "I must admit that until

now you were on the list. I didn't know how far you'd go to stop the chapel from being built."

She laughed softly. "My, my, Mr. Ramsgill."

"Jamie, please."

"Yes, Jamie. Then tell me why you suspect Franco. You can't be serious."

She got up and poured us each a drink. She sipped her Cinzano silently while I explained about the wine taken from the cellar the day Richard was killed and about the maid's testimony regarding the missing corkscrew. And about his opportunity.

"Could you think of a motive Franco would have for the murders?" I asked when I had finished.

Her face formed a blank stare.

"Not at all," she replied.

I set my glass of vodka on the coffee table.

"I want to find that missing bottle of wine," I said. "I've searched the architects' pavilions as well as I can without arousing suspicion, but I came up with nothing."

"Wait a minute," she said slowly, at the same time rising to her feet. Without speaking she rested her hand on my shoulder, steadying herself as she slipped back into her shoes. She took my glass and returned it with hers to the kitchen. Upon her return, she said:

"Professor, this may just be your lucky day."

We made for the courtyard. She took me by the hand and led me like a lost child back down below the walls of the villa and onto a narrow dirt path that wound its way through the woods. Snaking alongside the high rusticated stone wall beneath the pavilions, we soon came to a point that I recognized from the video.

"This is where I was yesterday," she said. "I could be wrong, but I think that I saw a bottle over here. And that's rare. Because Father pays a great deal of money to keep the villa grounds spotless."

She hurried me to a small set of steps, steps that led up to what appeared to be a sitting area, no more than a lichen-covered marble bench set up against a tree. She walked behind the bench while I stood with hands on hips, trying to catch my breath. She was in incredible condition.

"Here!" she yelled.

I quickly made my way over to her. She was picking something up from the ground, sticking the tip of her middle finger into the spout so as not to disturb the surface of the bottle. I hardly had to look at the familiar rooster on the neck of the bottle to identify it as Chianti. She turned it so I could see the label, and indeed it was. Chianti. Chianti Antinori. And the label was too fresh to have been in the weather very long.

"It's the bottle Cavalliere took from the cellar on Saturday," I said. "I'm almost sure of it."

She set the bottle upright on the ground.

"What do we do now?" she asked.

I turned and raised my eyes to the pavilions above us. I had the odd sensation that this was all too easy, that there was more to it than simply finding a missing bottle of wine.

"I suppose we should hide the bottle until Inspector Anghini comes," I said. "We'll take it to my pavilion."

"Do you think he'll believe you?" she asked.

"Facts don't lie," I said. "We now have the wine log, the bottle, the missing corkscrew and the fact that Sir Colin's door had been locked from the outside. The only thing we don't have is the typewriter that Sir Colin's suicide note was typed on and whatever was used to strangle him."

"Let's search Franco's room," she said, a sense of wild danger flashing in those big eyes.

"I think it would be better just to wait," I said. "Anghini should be here soon. Let them do the searching."

"No," she said. "I'm going whether you want to or not."

She scampered back down the path.

"Wait!" I said. "You can't go alone."

"Then you'd better come with me."

"Okay," I said. "I'll go. But we have to be careful. And I want to put this bottle in a safe place."

I took the bottle and we left the woods, making our way to the garden, where we dropped off the bottle at my pavilion. She then took me to the third floor of the main house, behind tiny attic windows, where up a back stairway on the garden side we quietly approached Cavalliere's quarters.

"How do you know he's not here?" I whispered.

"I don't," she replied. She didn't seem to care either.

"What if he catches us?" I asked. Creeping around the room of someone who had murdered two people didn't leave me feeling too optimistic at the consequences of being caught.

"I can handle Franco, Jamie. Leave it to me."

She approached his door, stopped and took a long breath. She then rapped lightly.

"He's not here," she said, after getting no answer.

"Are you sure you want to do this?" I asked.

"Me?" she replied. "I'm not going in. *You* are. While you search, I'll be out here keeping watch. If he comes back, I'll detain him."

"Thanks a lot," I said.

"Now go," she said. "We're wasting time."

Suddenly she kissed me. It surprised the hell out of me, but without hesitation I reached around her thin waist and pulled her to me. Her breasts pressed snugly against my chest. Her lips parted as I pressed my own against them. She was sweet and warm. I gently pulled away.

"Is that a bribe?" I said.

She swallowed and gave me a demure smile.

I returned the smile, then reached down and turned the doorknob. Our eyes continued to dance as I stepped inside and closed the door behind me.

Cavalliere had two rooms en suite, connected by a tall archway. On one side of the archway was the living area, and on the other a place to sleep. Off the bedroom were two doors, one to a large bathroom and the other to an ample closet. The walls of the living room and bedroom were of crimson damask and appointed with small paintings in gilded frames. The furniture was a mix of antique and Piruzzi, and the whole effect was that of a gentlemen's pied-à-terre, rather than quarters for a household servant.

I stepped into the bedroom and found a typewriter on a mahogany desk. It was electric, like those in the competitors' pavilions, but it was made by a different manufacturer and I suspected was somewhat older.

I pulled the note I had typed on Sir Colin's typewriter from my pocket and inserted it into Cavalliere's machine. I scrolled to a point just below my earlier typing and typed a similar message. Pulling it from the roller, I found it was evident immediately that the type on the two machines differed. So did the margin settings. I couldn't be sure, but it appeared at first glance that Cavalliere's machine typed more like the note found at the time of Sir Colin's death. I folded the paper and stuffed it into my vest.

I searched around me for anything else of interest. A small door led to his bathroom, and I stepped inside. There was nothing there except the normal accoutrements of a gentleman's bath, and the vestigial scent of cologne.

Back in the bedroom I combed through desk drawers and searched among his shelves. I searched tabletops and checked under the bed. In his sitting room I checked the closet, then after one last long look around, I started for the door. It was then that I heard something from the corridor. It was the sound of footsteps, muffled by carpet, but unmistakable, the sound of someone climbing the stairs at the end of the hall. I then heard his voice.

"Elena, what are you doing here?" It was Cavalliere. And he didn't sound too happy.

I stiffened and my adrenaline turned on like a faucet.

"I was looking for you," she said in a composed voice. "I . . . I need your help with something."

"What?"

His voice was deep and rigid. Elena had been so sure of herself earlier. I now hoped that she would come through.

"I want to move some furniture in my living room and I'd like you to help me."

"Of course," he said. "Let me get out of this uniform. I'll be right over."

He must have then reached for the doorknob, because the brass knob turned a few degrees. I positioned myself in the corner behind the door, but the jamb was too close to the wall to keep me hidden should he come inside. I found I was short of breath.

"It's just some small things I want moved," she said. "Nothing heavy. You can come as you are."

He was silent. I began to imagine him thinking it odd that Elena was positioned outside his doorway. He was on to us, I thought. I stopped breathing altogether.

"But just let me change, Elena. It won't take but a moment."

"Dinner's soon, Franco. You'll just have to change again in fifteen minutes if you do so now."

"But—"

"Come on . . ." she said in a high-pitched voice. She was walking away from the door. I imagined those foggy eyes of hers trained upon his, trying to coax him along. It was a gamble.

My own eyes were stuck to the doorknob.

"As you wish," he said softly.

And then slowly, like the second hand sweeping across the face of a clock, the doorknob returned to its original position.

I heard them walk away.

I stood motionless until I was sure that they were gone. I then started to leave, but before doing so I caught sight of another typewriter, this one lying in the corner of the room. It was like those that were in the pavilions. I wondered what Cavalliere was doing with it.

I then remembered that he was in charge of supplying the architects with their utensils. I realized that it must be Borromini's. Because he was using the quill pen, he would have had it removed by Cavalliere. Above the typewriter, standing upright in the corner, was a parallel edge. I walked over and picked it up. It was the same model as used by all of the architects except for Borromini, who used a T-square. Cavalliere, of course, would have retrieved it, too. I gently set it in the corner and was on my way out when another thought came to mind. Turning back towards the parallel edge, I noticed that its wire was missing. It was the same kind of wire that Sir Colin had hung from. The same kind of wire that had put an additional set of marks on his neck.

TWELVE

A pair of soaring steel-gray construction cranes were poised at the edge of the pavilions' garden, the largest one of the two with its boom extended over the villa walls. It raised a solid iron cylinder about the size of a fifty-gallon drum purposefully up a cable attached to its boom. When the cylinder reached a height equal to the group of architects standing at the edge of the overlook, the crane released the cylinder, dropping it straight down with the accelerating force of gravity towards the hillside below. Leaning beyond the balustrade, I watched with uneasy curiosity as the cylinder collided in a tumult with a sheet of steel piling, producing a horrendous pounding noise that rang in my ears like two freight trains colliding within a few feet of my head. The crane then lifted the cylinder again and repeated the procedure several times, raising and dropping it with the insistent rhythm of some magnificent giant piston. The pounding continued until my ears felt as if they were on fire, until I could take it no more, and just as I was about to scream, I peered down, and there, hemmed in by the sheet pilings that were being driven into the ground as foundations for Piruzzi's chapel, I saw my own body, stripped naked, my arms pinned against the ground, my enlarged brown eyes shifting in horror each time the giant steel drum dropped to within a few feet of my head. I could see sweat beading from my forehead like a dishrag being wrung out, and then suddenly, I sensed a black object above me, breathing slow deliberate breaths. I could hardly get my own breath it seemed, and I was cold, which was odd, because the air was quite warm. It was as though I were separated from the world around me, and although my mouth was wide open I couldn't get air. A familiar voice mentioned that the black object above me was seven times the size of the architects, almost as large as the cranes, and suddenly it was sucking all of the oxygen out of the atmosphere. The pounding continued, and the landscape got darker, as the shadow of the object enveloped everything within my view. It became so dark that I could no longer see, like a tornado enveloping the horizon. Nothing. Just the noise. And the cold. And the terrible lack of air.

"Jamie, wake up."

My eyes shot open, and I looked up to see the black object above me, but it was no longer seven times the height of a man. It was the size it was supposed to be, and it had a familiar smell to it, and long dark hair that fell down towards me like a cascading waterfall.

"Elena, what happened? Where am I?"

"You're in your room."

I now sensed another smell, this one familiar too. The unmistakable odor of natural gas.

I sat up anxiously and looked around. I now recalled falling asleep on the couch in my living room. I rubbed my eyes, which burned with the dry irritation that comes from lack of sleep, and I let them adjust to the light. Across the room, brightened by the late afternoon sun that streamed through the open terrace doors, was my Pullman kitchen. In the middle of a row of cabinets was a gas stove with an oven below.

"Do you smell gas?" I said.

"Yes, but it's almost gone," Elena said. "I opened all the doors and windows. What did you do, anyway? Start to boil water for tea and then fall asleep?"

I looked again at the range. There was a tea kettle on the stove that I had never seen before.

"I don't drink tea," I said. "How'd you get in here?"

"The front door," she said. "I must have knocked for five minutes. I finally came in, thinking something might be wrong."

I recalled the pounding in my dream. I now realized that it was Elena's knocking.

"I thought the door was locked," I said.

She sat down next to me and pulled my groggy head to her shoulder.

"Jamie, I think you're losing it. You do need sleep if you think the door was locked."

I raised my head abruptly from her shoulder and walked to the terrace doors. I stepped out and inhaled some fresh air. I then turned back to her.

"Somebody was here, Elena. Don't you see? I didn't turn on the gas and I'm sure that I locked the door."

"But who?"

"Where's Cavalliere?" I said.

"I left him twenty minutes ago."

My eyes skirted the room like a pool ball bouncing off bumpers. Suddenly, for the first time since arriving at the villa, I was scared. Damn scared. I was fearful before, not so much for myself, but for the others. Somehow, the earlier murders didn't seem threatening to me personally. But now, there was someone who knew that I was on to something; trying to gas me didn't fit the pattern of the seven sacraments. The deaths of Richard and Sir Colin were premeditated, even cleverly thought out. This was something else. A preemptive strike to quiet me. But who even knew I was investigating?

I walked slowly back to the couch and dropped to a cushion.

"Do you think it was him?" Elena asked.

I leaned back and considered the question. I had not seen Elena since Cavalliere's room. I had returned to my pavilion to collect my thoughts, reviewing notes to see if there was a hole in my logic. There had been a slight reticence in my mind regarding Cavalliere, but I really couldn't put a finger on why. I suppose I still couldn't figure out what had motivated him to kill. There had to be a motive. No money was missing, and Cavalliere had nothing to gain from Garbutt or Battle's not being in the competition. He knew neither of them well enough to have a personal vendetta against them, at least as far as I knew. There was of course the possibility that he was simply carrying out Piruzzi's orders, but there was also the way that everything seemed so obvious, almost as if he wanted to be found out. But now, after my nap and with a head intoxicated by gas, I didn't know what to think.

"I don't know," I said. "All I know is that I . . . we . . . have to be more careful. I don't think we can trust anyone."

I was talking with trepidation in my voice. Elena sensed my fear and put her arm around me.

"How'd it go with Cavalliere after you left me, anyway?" I asked.

"Fine," she said. "He suspects nothing."

"He must suspect something," I contradicted. "Or at least somebody does. And it's obvious that whoever it is doesn't want me around."

"What did you find in his rooms?" she asked.

I explained to her about his typewriter and about the parallel edge with the missing cable.

"So it must be him. I can't believe it. I've always been so fond of him."

"It is hard to believe," I said. "I mean what kind of motive could he possibly have? The other architects . . . *that* I could understand."

"But what other explanation is there?" she said. "At least if he's arrested, there will be an investigation. Right?"

I nodded.

"Then let's go find Father."

She rose and lifted me by the hand. As our eyes met, she stared back with the kind of wistful look that I had long since forgotten. The look unlocked memories of earlier times in my life when the sight of an attractive woman stirred me deeply, and what it is like to have those feelings requited. I suddenly felt embarrassed, but not because I found myself drawn to her. I was embarrassed because I now realized that I had spent the better part of the last decade pursuing an intellectual dream, at the same time neglecting the most fundamental of emotions. Not that my profession has somehow been unfulfilling, but rather, I suppose, deficient in the whole. In my narrow world among the stacks of rare books and research papers that clutter the desk of my dusty little office at the university, I had ignored what it's like to feel love. From time to time I've found some minor interest in a female colleague, or even on occasion met someone outside my own field via a chance encounter, but usually, it seems, I refused to be seduced. In my mind love was always something for people who had more time on their hands than I do. I had places to go and worlds to conquer, and the thought of being dragged down by a companion was one that simply had no appeal.

But everything seemed different now. Natural. I couldn't say honestly if it was because I was several thousand miles from home, or the fact that fear made me want to hold on to something solid. In the short time that I had known her, Elena had certainly not dragged me down. As I stared into the most fetching eyes that I had ever seen, I decided that I should try to make up for lost time.

I followed her out to the garden. We strolled slowly up towards the house, enjoying our brief moment of calm together, staying beneath the colonnade on the side of the garden that faced the lake. Before reaching the dining terrace we paused to take in the view. Off to our right, towards the deep blue basin cradled by mountains that was the magnificent lake, another day was coming to an end. Against the light blue dome of dusk, the setting sun was casting an iridescent glow on the underside of distant cumulus clouds. The sun was a brilliant ball of orange, like the intense embers of a fire when the flame is gone and all of the fire's energy is focused on the coals. It painted the lower parts of the clouds fire red, clouds that were otherwise mauve and purple, thick and grand. The clouds diminished in size as they reached the mountainous horizon and finally, creating a backdrop to the whole, a curtain of gray thunderheads could be seen beyond, the leading edge of a storm.

I heard a loud guttural meow and turned back towards the garden. The peafowl were restless, strutting around nervously, several of the cocks ruffling up their feathers. They were alternating calls, in volleys back and forth to one another like a tennis match. I glanced up towards the house and saw Paolo Liserio, the chef, approaching.

"Good evening, Paolo," said Elena.

"Good evening, Signorina Elena and Signor Ramsgill."

He was dressed in a stained, double-breasted white shirt and gray slacks, a crisp white toque perched upon his exuberant hair. I nodded and returned my eyes to the view. The dark clouds were building, forcing the blue out of the sky.

"Good for the moment," I said.

"Ah yes," he said. "The *pavoni,* they know when a storm is approaching." He turned and nodded towards the peafowl.

"We're ready for dinner," he continued. "The others are already assembled."

His tone was polite, but he emphasized the word "ready" to let us know that we were delaying the meal.

"Of course," I said. "By the way, Paolo, did you ask Franco about the bottle of wine he logged out of the cellar on Saturday?"

His gaze intensified as if he had forgotten my request. Then he smiled.

"Oh yes, yes, that," he said. "I almost forgot. Franco says he didn't do it. I showed him the log and he claimed that it wasn't his writing."

Though this wasn't the explanation I had hoped to hear, it did reinforce my impression of the sloppiness with which Cavalliere had covered his tracks.

"I think he's telling the truth," Liserio continued. "He has no reason to lie. One simple bottle of Chianti. It's not as if it were a valuable bottle. Besides, the *dottore* lets him take any wine for himself that he wishes."

He did have a reason to lie, but I couldn't tell Liserio that. On the other hand, I still found it perplexing that he had recorded it in the first place.

"Okay," I said, looking at Elena. "Thank you."

Liserio excused himself. We followed him up to the house and into the dining room. There we found Piruzzi standing at the end of the large elliptical dining table, surrounded by the four remaining architects in the competition.

I walked around the table and approached a seat that Piruzzi had kept for me next to him. Before I could reach it, however, Akio Hara stepped in front of me with a look of concern in his dark green eyes.

"Professor Ramsgill," he said in a near whisper. "Come to my pavilion after dinner." He pressed a folded piece of paper into my palm. I started to speak, but he left me for the end of the table, and I realized that he didn't want to be overheard.

I took my seat next to Piruzzi, who was now engaged in conversation with Thornburgh Keller, to his left. I unfolded my linen napkin and placed it in my lap. Beneath the napkin I carefully unfolded the paper Hara had given me and read it: "Keller tried to bribe me" was all it said. I stole a look at Hara, who sat opposite me, next to Elena. I could tell that he knew I was looking, but he wouldn't return my gaze. I stuffed the paper into my pocket.

"I need to speak with you," I said to Piruzzi a moment

later, once I could gain his attention. "About developments."

I assumed that he knew I meant developments regarding the murders. The way I said it, though, the others could have thought I was speaking of the competition. Keller leaned forward and looked at me around Piruzzi.

"Yes, yes," said Piruzzi. "You can tell me how my friend Thornburgh is faring. Along with the others."

Keller seemed to be hoping that I would say something about his design. His dim eyes strained to see me in the candlelight, with no regard for discretion.

Just then a flash of lightning lit up the silk curtains in brilliant fashion, the black grid of the window mullions standing out in stark contrast to the yellow-white illumination of the draped fabric. Keller's body stiffened and his eyes widened like those of a frightened child. I took a sip of wine and smiled to myself, wondering how someone like Keller had ever gotten so far in life. How much had he offered Hara to throw the competition, I wondered. No doubt that's what had transpired.

Thunder crashed in the distance, rumbling off like an unbridled horse.

"Renzo," I said once the noise had subsided. "Where's the inspector?"

Piruzzi stretched for his glass, blocking Keller's view.

"Let's be quiet about that in front of the others," he said, giving me a stern look.

He seemed upset, but I was getting impatient. Up until now I had bent to his wishes. I had agreed to inform him about what I knew, and I had even agreed, implicitly at least, to keep what I knew from the others. But that was before someone tried to kill me, too, and as the storm intensified outside, my anger was also rising. I was tired of all the bullshit, and as my eyes shifted to Cavalliere, standing in the corner of the room, I pressed on. The thunder continued to rumble. The wind picked up, now gusting, and it created a continuous rattle of the window sashes.

"The murders," I said in a voice that I knew would not be overheard, given the approaching storm. "I want to talk. And I want to see Anghini. We've waited long enough."

Piruzzi scooped a forkful of pasta into his mouth and ignored my plea.

"Renzo, I'm serious. I think I know who it is."

The lightning came again, this time followed by a thunderous crack, the villa now engulfed by the tempest. The sound of thick hard raindrops slapped at the panes of the dining room windows. I stared at Piruzzi, trying to gain his attention, but he didn't stare back. Cavalliere circled the table, pouring more wine.

"I found the empty bottle," I said when Franco had finished and returned to the corner of the room. "It was taken from the cellar on Saturday. The day Richard died."

I was talking loudly now, and the rainstorm pounded at the south side of the house.

"And the typewriter that the note was typed on. I think I know whose it is."

Still no reaction.

I gazed over toward Elena, as if I could silently communicate my growing frustration that Piruzzi showed no interest in what I was telling him. I looked toward Cavalliere, who now, in light of what I knew, appeared as a big dangerous animal. I glanced at Keller and Clissac, who both seemed upset at the storm. The rain continued to pound.

The main course was brought in, *piccione arrosto.* Piruzzi ate in silence, oblivious to my revelations. The others ate solemnly, with sidelong glances toward the storm. Cavalliere hovered over us like a prison guard, and I wondered what Piruzzi's reaction would be to my accusation that it was his majordomo. I was nervous considering the danger I thought we were in, the others nervous, it seemed, because of the impending deadline for the competition. The lightning continued, with hardly an interval between what were now the most violent of lightning strikes. The sound was deafening, exploding through the thin mountain air like an artillery barrage.

Three-quarters of the way through the meal, Piruzzi stood and made a few remarks to the group about the competition. He reiterated how the designs would be due in the morning, and how he was so looking forward to seeing the work the architects had produced. When he was finished, Pet Clissac, who had been keeping a nervous eye on the windows, rose without saying a word and left the room by the terrace doors. I looked over to the *dottore* and considered his rules for the competition. The group was to stay together for dessert and coffee before returning to work. But he showed no sign that Clissac's action had upset him.

A moment later Borromini rose and set his napkin on the table. He glanced at Renzo and excused himself. I suppose he expected a response, but without getting one he too quietly departed, presumably to return to work. Keller followed, and finally Hara, who, ever the gentleman, bowed to the *dottore* before exiting.

One of the servants then appeared from the kitchen. A moment later Liserio stood at the door. It was difficult to hear what he was saying, but he was clearly upset that his dinner had been abandoned.

"Don't be alarmed, Paolo," Piruzzi said, wiping his mouth and not bothering to turn towards his chef. "It's not your food. Everything was delicious, as usual. The architects, it seems, have performed an insurrection, realizing that they have but until tomorrow morning to finish their work."

Liserio nodded.

"Paolo," Piruzzi continued. "Do you have your car?"

"Yes."

"Forget the meal, even the dishes. It's a terrible night. Take the others and head home."

"But Dottore—"

"Do as I say. Franco can help us with anything else we need."

Liserio returned to the kitchen and two servants came out to clear the table. A few minutes later Liserio appeared again.

"We're going then," he said.

"Yes, yes. And be careful on the road."

The kitchen door swung on its pivot hinges and we heard them disappear through the back corridor.

"Ramsgill," Piruzzi said once they were gone. "You have vied for my attention all evening. The others are gone now. I'm ready to hear what you have to say."

I looked toward Elena, who nodded furtively. Cavalliere still stood somewhere over my right shoulder.

"Okay," I said, gathering my thoughts. "Let's see. Hara's got a brilliant scheme. Many of his drawings are done. The others, however, still have a lot—"

Piruzzi pushed himself away from the table, the groan of his chair interrupting my train of thought.

"I don't want to hear about the competition," Piruzzi said impatiently. "I think all of us in this room know that you suspect murder."

I thought of the consequences of telling what I knew. In the movies, the killer is always brought to task at the end, and he usually does something desperate. Would Cavalliere do the same? Where in the name of God and Mary was Anghini?

"Well, it's complicated," I said, trying to stall for time. I began to play with the rim of my wineglass.

Piruzzi gave me the second unpleasant look I had seen from him.

"It's just that . . . shouldn't we call Anghini? I'll tell what I know when he arrives."

"You'll tell what you know now," Piruzzi said adamantly. "We had an agreement. You tell me what you know before talking to the inspector."

Cavalliere cleared his throat. It was a deep resonant sound from a neck as thick as a sewer pipe.

"Maybe we *should* wait," Elena said, realizing my predicament.

"You stay out of this," Piruzzi snapped at his daughter.

Again he looked at me with hard eyes. Thunder was crashing around us and water could be heard cascading off the garden steps to the hillside below the villa. The wind rushed through cracks in the doors and windows with the force of compressed air.

I had no choice but to speak. When I opened my mouth, I found it talking without consulting my brain.

"Could you ask Franco to leave?" I said.

Cavalliere's massive shoulders tightened. He started to speak but Piruzzi didn't give him a chance.

"Do as Professor Ramsgill says," he ordered.

Cavalliere stood like a bull. His nostrils flared and his warm eyes seemed to darken. He stayed long enough to let us know that he wasn't happy with my request, but he then disappeared into the library.

Piruzzi turned to me immediately and asked for an explanation. I explained what Elena and I had discovered about the wine bottle, the corkscrew, the typewriter, even the parallel edge. He sat expressionless before downing an almost full glass of wine. He then pushed himself away from the table and started to speak.

Just as he opened his mouth we were interrupted by a terrible sound. A blood-curdling scream came from across the garden, pounded by the rain into a dull echo by the time it reached us, but nevertheless a scream. We sprang from the table and ran to the terrace, staring out into the dark downpour, trying desperately to sense its source. I could see Thornburgh Keller at the south end of the garden, standing in the light of Gio Borromini's open doorway. Keller was drenched from the rain, and upon seeing us he pointed into Borromini's pavilion. I took off ahead of Renzo and Elena and reached the doorway even before Keller. Leaving a trail of soaked footprints in my wake I dashed down the corridor to Borromini's bedroom, where I found him lying on the floor, gasping for breath, shattered glass about him, and a wash basin turned upside down on the carpet. There was water everywhere.

"Gio!" I yelled. I grabbed him by the collar and pulled his face up next to mine. His eyes were wild with terror and his face a purplish color, and he breathed in heavy gasps. Water beaded off his convulsing face as if it were boiling. I tore open his shirt and lifted his arms overhead, pulling up on his torso in an attempt to relieve pressure on his chest.

The gasping continued. I thrust my hand into his mouth, thinking that he was choking on something, but he pulled back from me shaking his head violently from side to side to signal that he wasn't. I looked up to the others, who now stood beside me at the bed, and I shook my head to signal that I didn't know what to do. I held him stationary and pleaded with him to hang on. He continued convulsing and I was sure that we were losing him, but at some point after what seemed like forever, his breathing changed its rhythm and his convulsing stopped. He appeared to be returning to normal. Finally his breathing slowed and became less raspy, and he leaned against the bed on his own power. He weakly picked up his broken glasses from the carpet and fumbled to get them onto his face.

"Drown me . . ." he gasped once he finally calmed down. "Someone tried to drown me."

"My God," said Keller, who was as white and pasty as powdered lime. Elena and Piruzzi stood silent with a look of terror in their eyes.

"Who?" I said.

"Don't know," he gasped. "I was washing my face at the basin. . . . Must have had my head in the water when someone came from behind me. He shoved me deeper into the basin and held me there until I could no longer breathe. Somehow I was able to get a vase from the table and break it over his head."

A cobalt blue vase had shattered into scores of pieces surrounding him on the floor. The glass was thick and the blow to his assailant must have been a heavy one. The basin lay in the middle of the glass, white enamelware dented on one side. It must have been knocked to the floor in the struggle. There was no other evidence. The attacker had to have left by the front door, because it was open when we arrived.

Just then Cavalliere appeared in the bedroom. He was breathing hard and took one look at Borromini and his Adam's apple rose and fell. A bolt of lightning lit the air, followed immediately by the shattering sound of thunder. And then another scream.

I looked at Piruzzi in horror. The sound had come from across the garden.

I stood.

"Where's Hara?" I said. "And Clissac?"

No one knew the answer.

I instinctively started for the door.

"Franco," Piruzzi ordered. "Go with him."

I'm sure Piruzzi's thought was well intentioned, but Cavalliere was the last person in the world that I wanted to leave that pavilion with. There was no time to protest, however, and Franco quickly followed me out.

We dashed over to Hara's door, and as rain sheeted off the cornice of his pavilion, we hugged the face of the building. Franco beat at the door, pounding hard with fists the size of softballs. There was no answer, and as it was locked, once again, we had no choice but to break it down.

We took turns, and after a few moments we fell into the warm and dry foyer. Immediately, a distinctive odor overwhelmed us. The pavilion was silent and we had no way of knowing where Hara was. We ran upstairs, but the studio was empty. Back downstairs, the bedroom was empty too. The door to the bathroom was closed, but the air outside it was moist and warm. I knocked several times. There was no answer. I opened the door slowly and stepped into a steam-filled room. The odor was now pungent, a combination of a wet clean smell with something burnt and sour. I couldn't see anything, but I then moved towards what I thought was the tub. Soon the steam escaped into the bedroom and I was able to see that the shower curtain was closed across the front of the tub. I approached cautiously and slowly pulled it back.

Akio Hara was slumped across the bottom of the tub, his nude body lifeless, his pale skin spotted with red welts, his hair matted and kinked, thinned to a point that he looked almost bald. A thick yellowish liquid coated both him and the white tiled wall next to the tub, and from somewhere within the odd mix of odors I was smelling, one smell overpowered the others. It was the odor of burnt flesh. I turned my attention to the shower head, which was not running, but which dripped some of the liquid. I touched it with the tip of my finger. It was hot to the touch and it rolled off my finger to the tub below.

"Unction," I mumbled in a stunned voice. I thought of Hara's earlier fear, and of my inaction on his behalf. I could have told him the truth. He didn't deserve this.

"What?" Cavalliere asked.

"He's been boiled in hot oil," I said.

Cavalliere didn't respond.

"The water is still turned on," Cavalliere said in a voice as full of trauma as my own. "But nothing's coming out."

It was true. He leaned over and turned the lever handles of the hot and cold faucets off. He looked at Hara and shook his head. Without saying a word he backed out of the bathroom. He turned and I heard him walking down the corridor back towards the garden. He stopped and opened a door. His inquisitiveness belied my idea that he was the killer.

I joined him in the front hall. He was standing at the open door of a closet beneath the stairs to the second floor. He pulled on a light chain and the contents of the closet were revealed. Cleaning supplies mostly, a few boxes of light bulbs, and in the back left-hand corner a small water heater. The supplies in that area had been pushed aside, and at the floor, attached to the bottom of the water heater, was a contraption that looked for all intents and purposes like a miniature old-fashioned water tower. It consisted of a glass jug of perhaps ten-gallon capacity held upside down by wooden supports. The structure was made up of doweled truss members, all on a small scale, and they reminded me of the construction of a model railway bridge. A copper tube lead from the bottom of the jug to the heater's water intake line. Within the jug was what appeared to be a weighted float, and the float in turn was attached to a steel cable that ran through a hole in the top of the jug and then via a pulley across to the thermostat on the water heater. The thermostat was set at one hundred degrees centigrade. That was enough to boil someone alive, or at least to induce cardiac arrest.

I knelt next to the mechanism. I was feeling nauseous.

"Simple," I said in a weak voice. "The water line intake was shut off so that the only liquid entering the system was oil. Oil being lighter than water means that it rose to the top of the heater's tank. It must have worked like a siphon. When the water ran out the faucets flowed with oil, but not before the oil jug emptied, tripping the thermostat. Hara would've been taking a normal shower when all of a sudden the water changed to oil and simultaneously heated up to a point that it would kill him. He probably never knew what hit him. And no telling how long this thing has been in the closet. A machine for death."

It was an ingeniously sadistic construction. The kind of thing I imagined the Marquis de Sade taking pleasure in designing, but with a certain familiarity to it.

Just then another bolt of lightning charged the air, followed a split second later by a deafening burst of thunder. I caught a glimpse of Cavalliere's granite chin in the illumination, then suddenly the lights dimmed. He stood over me like a giant. A moment later the lights dimmed again, then they went out. I rose from the floor, and in the darkness, dashed out into the storm. I circled the trees and ran back into Borromini's now darkened pavilion.

"Elena!" I yelled. She was the only one I trusted.

I passed through the corridor and into the bedroom. It was dark and quiet, the only sound being the crushed shards of glass underfoot. Elena and the others were gone.

I then returned to the front door and saw Cavalliere standing like a robot in the rain. I hurried to the terrace doors of the main house and stepped inside. The dining room was dark now, but from the library a faint light emanated. I tiptoed towards the double doors until I could see Elena standing at the bar lighting candles. Keller sat like a zombie, wrapped in a wool blanket, in one of the overstuffed sofas. The room had an ethereal glow.

"Where's Renzo?" I asked. "And Borromini?"

Elena turned slowly.

"Father's getting Borromini a sedative. He's terribly shaken."

I walked over to the telephone, which was on the bar.

"How do I call the police?" I asked.

"Here, let me do it."

She set down her candle and took the phone. She started dialing and placed the receiver to her ear. Cavalliere then came into the room from the same direction that I had come. He sensed my fear and stood his ground in the corner.

"It's dead," she said, holding the receiver towards me.

I took it. There was no dial tone. I jammed the buttons in the receiver cradle but nothing happened.

"Of course," I said sarcastically. "This is great."

"We'll all be dead by morning," Keller said in a stupor. He looked as if he had aged a decade.

Just then Piruzzi walked into the room from the front hall. He was carrying a long candle that cast an upward light. It accentuated the fat on his lower face, and the glistening sweat on his brow.

"Where's Gio?" I asked.

"I've given him something to relax. He's lying on the sofa in my study."

"Is he okay?"

"He'll be fine. He just needs some rest."

Piruzzi placed his candle on the marble mantel.

"The phones are out," I said.

He walked over to where I was standing and tried to get a dial tone. Having no luck, he hung up the receiver.

"Hara's dead," I said. "Boiled alive, by hot oil."

Keller closed his eyes and pulled his feet up, getting himself into a fetal position. He rocked back and forth like an autistic child.

"How?" asked Elena.

"A gadget hooked up to his shower."

"No," she said. "Please no."

I walked to her side and placed my arm around her. But Piruzzi gave me a dismissing look, so I pulled away.

"How long do you think the power will be out?" I asked.

"Could be hours," Piruzzi replied. "Or days. We're isolated here. If one of the lines was hit on the mountain, they may not even know about it down in Salò."

Elena walked over to the window.

"It's hard to tell if the lights are on down there," she said. She was referring to the towns and villages around the lake.

"So we wait," I said. "And wonder who the killer is."

"Yes," said Keller. "And who'll die next."

My eyes rose to the ceiling. The candlelight undulated softly on the murals there, murals of beauty that had been twisted into the blackest of nightmares.

"That makes four of seven," I said in a monotone.

Elena and Renzo knew that I was talking about the seven sacraments, but Keller stopped rocking long enough to ask for an explanation.

"What?"

"The seven sacraments. The killer's using the seven sacraments as a leitmotif, macabre as that might be."

Keller lifted his eyes.

"Tell me about them," he said.

I explained their nature and how Piruzzi's ancestor Braegno had considered them important enough to put on the ceiling. Now centuries later a mad killer was using them to play out a twisted game of carnage.

"First there was Richard's death," I said, pointing to the communion panel. "A mock communion. He was found with bread and wine. I suppose Richard was the Christ figure. Had to die. Then there was confession. Sir Colin's fake suicide note was entitled "My Confession." Baptism was next, I suppose. A near deadly baptism for Borromini. Luckily unsuccessful. And finally Hara was anointed with oil. Extreme unction it's called in church doctrine. Though *boiling* oil isn't exactly what the church fathers had in mind."

"The murderer's moving up the garden," Keller said. "I'll be next."

He shook his head and sighed. I turned to the bar and dropped two ice cubes into a glass, then filled it halfway with vodka. I paused for a second, realizing that the killer had seven victims in mind. I downed the clear liquid, shook off a shiver, and set down the glass. It wasn't lost on me that I occupied one of the seven pavilions, and that someone had already paid me a visit. I didn't want to become the seventh sacrament.

"Our murderer has quite a sense of humor," I said wiping my lips with the back of my hand. "He's clever, too."

"A psychopath," Elena said bluntly.

"You say 'he,' Keller said to me. "Why not 'she'?" He removed his limp left hand from beneath the blanket and pointed in Elena's direction.

"Elena had nothing to do with the murders."

"And how do you know that?"

I explained how her alibi for Sir Colin's murder was on videotape.

"But she could've been involved with the others."

"I think that all of the attacks were by the same person," I said. "The seven sacraments links them. Besides, Elena was in the dining room with Renzo and me when Gio was attacked."

"And that rules you two out as well, I presume?"

"You figure it out."

Lightning lit up the window draperies, followed by thunder that now seemed to be moving away. I poured myself another drink and cradled the glass in my palm.

"So who's the killer? Seems as though you've been thinking about this."

My eyes turned to Cavalliere. He stood away from the warmth of the candlelight, in a shadowed eddy of the large room.

"The evidence leads to Franco," I said.

"What?!" he responded.

"What do you mean?" Keller asked.

"Richard Battle choked to death," I said to Cavalliere. "But the wine found in the glass next to him was not from the bottle on the table. It was a heavier wine. Like the one you took from the cellar on Saturday. A Chianti Antinori."

"Liserio asked me about that wine," Cavalliere said. "I wondered what he meant. The only wine I took from the cellar on Saturday were the bottles we had for dinner. I absolutely did not log out this wine you speak of."

He wiped his brow and his eyes shifted to Piruzzi, who now sat on the sofa next to Keller. Piruzzi evaded his gaze.

"Then who did?" I said. "The wine cellar stays locked. Also, a corkscrew was missing from the library that night. It mysteriously reappeared the following day."

"So?" he said.

"It was returned to the bar drawer as it's always returned by you."

"That's ridiculous."

"And in the case of both Richard's and Garbutt's deaths you were the first at the scene. Tonight, you were absent when Gio was attacked."

He moved like a slow rolling boulder in my direction.

"You don't know what you're talking about," he said. His eyes were now dark, and serious.

"And I have this," I said.

I pulled the samples of typing from my pocket.

"The bottom note was typed on your typewriter. I think it matches the fake suicide note."

"How did you get that?"

"From your room."

He looked again at Piruzzi.

"*Dottore*, this is an outrage!"

Piruzzi shrugged.

"Let's tie him up," Keller said.

I looked at Keller in amazement.

"You tie him up," I said, considering the task. "As long as we're here together, we're safe. Besides, I said the evidence leads to Franco. I didn't say I was sure."

"How sure do you need to be?" Keller asked. "Want him to slit somebody's throat in full view of everyone?"

I tossed back a fair portion of my drink.

"It might be you who'd do the slitting," I said.

Keller's eyes widened. He pulled his blanket tighter around his frail frame.

"You're not suggesting," he said in a distinctly lock-jaw voice, "that *I* am a suspect?"

"Perhaps," I said.

"On what grounds?"

"On the grounds that you tried to bribe Hara into dropping out of the competition. And you also tried to blackmail me."

Piruzzi looked up with interest.

"What?" he said.

I pulled the paper Hara had given me at dinner from

my pocket and handed it to Piruzzi. He, in turn, handed it to Keller.

"Hara gave me that," I said. "Can you deny it?"

"Yes. Well, no, but that means nothing! Just because I tried to influence someone doesn't mean I would murder him. And do you think a man of my size and age had the strength to hang Garbutt? It's ludicrous, Ramsgill!"

His face was red, and his old eyes fiery.

"I don't think you'd stop at anything to win the competition," I continued. "And as far as your strength goes, men have been known to do superhuman things when they're desperate. And bankruptcy will make someone desperate."

His face had contorted into a fixed frown.

"You have no evidence," he said in a calmer voice. "Cavalliere's your killer. Or what about Clissac, for God's sake?"

For the first time since the commotion in the garden I realized that Clissac was missing. She had left us abruptly in the middle of the storm, and in the confusion we had simply forgotten her.

"Where's Pet?" asked Elena. Her voice was filled with agitation.

"The last time I saw her was at dinner," Renzo said.

I got a bad feeling in my gut. Where had she been the entire time? I recalled her nervousness during dinner. What was it she knew? My mind circumvented all that I had just said about Cavalliere and Keller. I found myself wondering whether Clissac was the murderer—or had she simply been the next victim? Either way I felt that I had to find out. I set down my unfinished drink and started for the door.

THIRTEEN

"I'm going to look for her," I said.
"Jamie, no."

I turned to Elena, whose eyes were full of worry. Her concern comforted me, but it didn't change my resolve.

"I'll be okay. Just don't let anyone leave the room. As long as you're all together, then everyone's safe. I won't be long."

She started to protest again, but Piruzzi quieted her. I couldn't tell if he was in agreement that I should go, or simply upset that she was displaying an interest in me. Sooner or later I would have to let him know how I felt about her, and I wondered what his reaction would be. He rose and put his arm around his daughter.

I walked out of the room with their two pairs of eyes fixed upon me.

Outside, the tumult had subsided, and as I stepped from the cover of the dining terrace, there was but a fine cool mist drifting down from the dark sky. The temperature had dropped. I could still hear cascading water, but it had slowed to a faint trickle. My shoes squeaked softly as I crossed the slippery cobblestones, the only sound in the now empty garden. I felt as though I was walking through a cemetery, the quiet pavilions like so many mausolea. For a moment I even wondered whether Braegno, Piruzzi's ancestor, might have intended them to be mausolea. They certainly could have passed for such on this damp horror-filled night.

I passed the pavilion of Garbutt and Battle, long since empty, then Hara's, with his body still inside. As I came to Clissac's, I heard something in the deep recesses of the arcade, a low hiss that I recognized as the sound of a peacock.

I stepped up to her door, paused, and looked around me. Death hung over the garden like a pall, and at that moment it seemed that the garden couldn't possibly ever again be filled with the beauty and light of our first day here. We had lost more than our colleagues in what had taken place. I felt I had lost the corner of my heart long reserved for Italy.

I turned the doorknob of Clissac's door and stepped inside. I had forgotten to ask Piruzzi for a flashlight, but I seemed to remember seeing one in the closet of Hara's pavilion. I hugged the wall of the foyer until I came upon the stairway, then worked my way to the closet beneath it. My grasping hands found a flashlight on an overhead shelf.

I turned it on and made a quick survey of the closet, confirming that there was nothing unusual about its contents. I then continued quietly down the hall. The bedroom was empty, clothes scattered about, the dead smell of cigarette smoke in the stiff air. The bathroom was also empty, populated only by toilet articles that lined a glass shelf above the sink. I looked in the tub and found nothing.

Upstairs had the same empty eeriness to it that the other pavilions had, when after the deaths of Sir Colin and Richard I searched their quarters. The studio was filled with Clissac's drawings for Piruzzi's chapel, and two days' worth of wadded up tracing paper. There was no sign of her, though, dead or alive, and something told me she had not been here for a while.

I stumbled back downstairs, the flashlight beam bouncing off the plaster walls. I paused in the hall, but before making for the front door, I shone the beam back towards the bedroom once more. I had not checked the balcony earlier, and though I didn't think I'd find anything there, I knew that I had to look.

Approaching the French doors with more than a little apprehension, I unlocked one of them and quietly stepped outside. A quick, silent search yielded nothing, so I returned to the bedroom, locked the door behind me, and started again for the foyer. It was then that I saw a scrap of paper resting atop the dresser that I hadn't noticed the first time around. I picked it up and placed it under my light. It was torn from a notebook, blue ink on folded yellow paper in a flowing hand. It read "Meet me tonight, my love."

I immediately thought of the man in the long coat whom Clissac had met late the night before. There was no way of telling when the note had been written, but I felt a desire to know who he was, or what he and Clissac were meeting for.

I returned outside and considered what to do next. I could make for the relative safety of the library to wait out the night, hoping like the others that help would be on the way. That would be the rational thing to do, but I found a curious intoxication coming over me, and the longer I stood in the vacant garden, the more strongly I believed that the enigma had to be unraveled. And for whatever reason, I was the one to unravel it. I wanted to know who the murderer was, and why the crimes had been committed. I wanted to know what, if anything, Clissac and the man had to do with the murders. Without considering it another moment, I found myself walking to the corner of the house, not towards the warm candlelight from within, but up the stairs that led to the forecourt, and through the gate piers that flanked the road.

I started down towards the small village, and as I walked, my mind expanded like the night sky. I mulled over every possible scenario for the crimes. I thought to myself how often my own suspicions had changed. The grounds on which I based my queries kept shifting, and each time I thought I was close to the real answer, the answer seemed to slip away. Cavalliere, Keller and Clissac—the three people on whom I now focused, were all capable of committing the crimes, and still in the back of my mind there was the curious personality of our host and the possibility that he had orchestrated it all. Though he was with me when Borromini had been attacked, I had the feeling that he knew more than he was letting on.

It was well after midnight when I reached the fork in the road where the cart path veered off to the right and skirted along the contours of the mountain towards the little village church. I paused for a moment and caught my breath while I considered what I would do if I encountered Clissac there. The fine mist that remained from the storm tickled my face. Given the fact that I didn't have a weapon, other than the flashlight, and that she and her friend would outnumber me, I only had the knowledge that I could possibly surprise them. Clissac was not a big woman and she was several years my senior. Hopefully, her male companion would be equally as old.

I started off again, and it wasn't long before the narrow passage through the woods widened and I reached the high garden wall that led to the church. I could hardly see the wall when I came upon it. I didn't want to use the flashlight for fear of giving myself away. I walked silently along the wall's sinuous form, using my ears as much as my eyes to guide me. The dull sound in my left ear confirmed its presence, and as long as I was on this line, I would ultimately arrive at my destination. I soon came upon a hollow sound, and in the bleak darkness I paused while my other faculties tried to sense where I was. I realized I was now at the cemetery gate, and that a few yards ahead of me was the church, its bulk rising before me like a black precipice. There were no lights on in the village.

At this point I had a decision to make. For if Clissac

were in the church as I suspected, then I could either go in through the front door, or if I remember correctly, through a side door that faced the cemetery. I decided upon the cemetery door, thinking back to my desire for the element of surprise. I cautiously touched the wet iron of the cemetery gate, which the night before had been secure. This time it wasn't locked, and I pulled easily on the heavy iron, which didn't squeak but just sort of groaned, and when I had it just far enough open that I could squeeze by, I stepped forward.

I heard the fluttering of wings from somewhere and I carefully closed the gate to behind me. I followed the small stone path that led through the cemetery, and in this lonely place I felt as isolated as any man on earth. I stepped prudently, not wanting to make a sound. I soon met a musty odor and stillness of air that I knew was the wall of the church. I clutched the unlit flashlight tightly, and with my free hand I reached ahead, taking one step at a time, until a moment later I came into contact with cool wet stucco. I then sidestepped, on what was now soft ground, ever so slowly until I reached the door. I pushed but it didn't budge.

I ran my fingers over its splintered surface and came upon the latch. Pulling the weight of the door towards me in order to relieve pressure on the latch bolt, I put my thumb down and pressed. The door opened quietly, but I held it stationary once it had reached a point just wide enough to let me slip in, so that my presence would not be revealed to anyone who might be inside. I listened for sounds that might be human. Not hearing any, I stepped in and closed the door behind me. An acrid odor hung in the air. It was as quiet and still inside as I had remembered from before, but now, without even so much as a foot-candle of light coming through the windows, I had a hard time getting my bearings. I stood motionless long enough to know that the nave was empty, then paced towards the center of the void.

I looked around me for a source of light, any source,

even a line from a door bottom that connected to an adjoining room. But there was nothing, nothing but black. The longer I stood there the more I sensed that Clissac wasn't around, for what would she be doing in darkness? I decided to use my light.

The flashlight punched through the darkness like a lighthouse beacon, sweeping across the dusty floor in an oval pool of warmth. I directed it until it reached the center of the nave, then shone it back towards the front door. Seeing nothing, I then turned to the rear of the church and raised the beam of light to the altar, where- upon on carpeted steps of burgundy, the white shaft fell onto a bulky mass beneath the cross, a crumpled sheet of greenish gold silk. Beside the mass was a pile of clothes.

My breathing slowed and I took a half-dozen steps forward. My throat tightened at the same time a wave of adrenaline rushed through my body. I stepped upon the first altar riser with my soggy shoe. Then the second. I stood above the sheet. I drew a long breath of the cool wet air, then reached down. I pulled back on the soft fabric until it slipped away onto the stairs.

The stiff lifeless bodies of Pet Clissac and the man were locked in a tight embrace. They were only partially clothed, she in a black lace bra and matching garter belt, and he in a pink oxford shirt. Their clutch looked like frozen passion.

He was a handsome man about her age, with long fingers, the tips of which lay softly across her cheek. His middle was losing its shape, but his skin hung tight upon his bony frame. His blue eyes, now foggy and moisture- less, stared into hers, and hers were similar, though full of pain. Their heads lay sideways on the altar floor, and into the temple of each, as if pinned by a spike and hammer, a small round impression, the mark of two single bullets that had ended each of their lives. There was very little blood.

Clissac's hair was pulled back in a bun, still damp from the rain. I thought back to her nervousness during the

meal. Her quick exit was precipitated by a desire to come
to the church to meet this man, the mystery man who it
now seemed, from the matching wedding bands on their
fingers, was her husband. Her condition at dinner was
concern for him, knowing that he would be waiting for
her, knowing that he would be caught in the rain, knowing that Piruzzi forbade any of the competitors to leave
the villa grounds, even if only to meet one's lover. I now
suspected Clissac had done the same the night before
when I had followed them here. But this time, her rendez-
vous had proved fatal, for what she didn't know—what
Piruzzi wouldn't allow me tell his guests—was that there
was a murderer at large. As I stood over the murderer's
fourth and fifth victims I felt the guilt that I had felt that
first night, when, thinking Richard had drunk himself to
death, I had failed to step in and help.

Clissac died for love. The promise of fame and wealth
might have lured her to the villa, but neither Piruzzi's
rules nor Piruzzi's deadline had kept her from meeting
her spouse to satisfy their desire. I wished that love had
such a hold over me, and that in the revulsion of this
night, I too had someone to cling to.

"The fifth of the seven sacraments," I muttered. "Matrimony."

I stepped away from the bodies and settled into a pew.
Turning out my light, I considered where to go from
here. I was disgusted. Clissac was no longer a suspect,
and at the rate I was going, there would be no suspects
left by the time it was just the killer and me. I was some
fucking detective.

What more did I know now, I wondered, than I had
known when I left the villa? I knew that the murderer had
a gun, and I knew that he would use it. I knew that the
murderer had come to this place, sometime between dinner and less than an hour ago.

I rose and walked back to Clissac's body. I pressed my
fingertips to her husband's groin and felt a slight warmth.
The air temperature hovered in the fifties, and inside the

little church it felt cooler still. Though I can't profess to know anything about the way a body cools after it expires, it did seem that if not close to normal body temperature, then Monsieur Clissac's groin was at least not far below it. I could only assume it meant that they had not been dead very long.

My muscles stiffened. Was the murderer still here? It then occurred to me that he must be at the villa, for less than an hour ago I was in the library with all of the suspects. But how could that be? If the suspects were all at the villa when Clissac and her husband were killed, then who did the killing? How could they possibly have been killed by someone who could not have made it to the church during the same time period that I had come?

I delved further back into my logic.

I knew that it wasn't Elena.

I didn't think it was Keller, because even though I had provoked him in the library, he truly wasn't strong enough to have killed Sir Colin. The only time he had been out of my sight during the entire evening was the period from the time he left dinner with the others until the time we heard Borromini scream. Less than fifteen minutes. That wasn't even enough time for a fleet-footed man to have come to the church and have murdered Clissac, much less Thornburgh Keller.

I returned to my pew and stared into darkness. The old wood creaked and the sound expanded into the void. The dark of the church was like the emptiness in my mind. Why didn't a solution come?

I turned my attention to Cavalliere, on whom I had directed so much suspicion. I tried to place him at different times during the night. He was with us in the dining room until just before Borromini screamed. He then joined us in Borromini's pavilion, not too long after. Not nearly enough time to have come here. From that point forward he was in my company. He went with me to Hara's pavilion, then soon joined us in the library. My suspicion of him was based upon so many obvious clues, but now, in retrospect, they seemed too obvious to be plausible. Someone had tried to set him up.

Piruzzi was next in my order of thinking, and he too had been in my sight almost the whole time. He stayed in Borromini's pavilion when Cavalliere and I went to check on Hara, but then appeared again in the library shortly after I got there. Not enough elapsed time to have done this. Besides, he was in the dining room with Elena and me when Borromini was attacked.

I pulled up my damp collar and tried to shake off a chill. Where did that leave me, I wondered. I went back over it again, then again, and the longer I sat there, the less clear it all became. It was like a shattered jigsaw puzzle whose pieces were scattered to the wind. Every alley I had gone up had turned into a dead end. What was it that was so obvious, but that appeared to be so clouded? Who could have even known that Clissac was here? I went back through each death, each event, that had led me to where I was now. It didn't hold together. Somewhere my logic had gone astray.

The stillness of the sanctuary contradicted the noise in my mind. My thoughts raced over every conceivable angle, and then even over some that weren't so conceivable. I felt as though I were in a dream, running fast but without ever going anywhere. I reviewed motives and opportunities, evidence found at the scene. I tried to picture each of them in the role of the murderer, and I even went back and reviewed why Elena couldn't be guilty. The dark wet air pressed heavily upon me, but my mind refused to be weighed down. I struggled with my tormented brain to find the answer. Where did it leave me, I asked it one more time.

And finally, the answer revealed itself.

FOURTEEN

It left me with Borromini.

I sat in the dark sanctuary thinking about Gio Borromini, architect of Rome.

A fundamental question echoed across my mind. How could he have been the murderer if he was almost murdered himself? There could be but one answer. He hadn't almost been murdered.

I thought back through the evening's events. Borromini, like the other architects, left dinner before it was over. We then heard his scream. His front door was open, but virtually no time had elapsed from the point that we heard the scream until we stood on the terrace and Keller pointed to his pavilion. How could his attacker have gotten out of there in such a short time? We came to his aid and stayed with him until we heard Hara. He stayed behind with the *dottore* and Elena, and I didn't see him after that. When I got to the library later, he was already in the *dottore*'s den under the effects of a sedative.

But what if he never took the sedative? Piruzzi joined us in the library, and from that time on, Borromini could have come here. I thought about Clissac's body temperature. She had not been dead long. But how could he have known she was here? I then recalled that after Clissac left in the middle of dinner that Borromini was next to go. Perhaps he caught up with her in the garden. Maybe she

even told him that she was coming here to meet her
husband.

A tree branch lapped at the windows and broke my
train of thought. I took a couple of deep breaths. There
was a humming sound somewhere in the near distance.

It must be Borromini then. I thought back to when we
had come to his aid. He said he had been washing his face
in the basin when someone attacked him from behind.
He almost drowned, he said, before breaking a vase over
his assailant's head. I tried to picture it, imagining myself
bent down in the basin, my arms in front of me, my head
thrust forward. If I could have grabbed the vase, I
thought, could I truly have broken it over my attacker's
head? He would have been behind me, and above me,
and the force required would have been great. I recalled
the vase. It was not one of those thin crystalline types,
but rather the glass was thick and it wouldn't have shattered easily. In fact, would it have shattered at all? And
then, an incongruity came to light.

If the vase was broken over his attacker's head, then
why was no one at the villa bleeding? In the least, why
was no one bruised? Maybe he didn't hit anyone at all.
Suppose he staged the whole thing, and did so just at the
moment that Hara was burned to erase suspicion from
himself? I pictured the hot oil contraption Cavalliere and
I had found in Hara's closet. I thought at the time that
there was something familiar about it. I now realized that
it resembled the fantastically Leonardesque machines
that Borromini drew. No electronic gadgets for him, just
old-fashioned torture devices.

I buried my burning eyes in my hands. The hum I was
hearing seemed to modulate, and the still air outside had
become the faintest breeze. The windows of the little
church seemed to whisper.

Where was he, I wondered. Suddenly I didn't feel safe
knowing that the suspects were at the villa, because the
suspect list was down to one and the others would be
thinking that Borromini was asleep in Piruzzi's den.

I noticed my mouth was dry.

I stood and started for the door of the church, walking briskly, hoping my mind would decide upon a course of action by the time I was outside. I opened the door and let the cool damp air work its way into the nave. I still heard the humming, and I stopped to consider its source. It was coming from a direction beyond the altar, and a quick flash of my light back through the dark sanctuary located a door. I found myself drawn towards it, not knowing exactly why. I made my way back down the nave and stepped around the bodies at the altar. I then turned off the flashlight and opened the door. Feeling my way to a set of stone steps, I descended until I came upon solid ground. I was in the church's crypt and could see nothing, but the humming was more insistent and I followed my ears.

I came upon another door and I stood before it wondering what to do. The sound was coming from within the next room, a rhythmic whir, low-pitched and constant. I was without anything resembling a weapon except for my light. I pushed forward and stepped into the room. The floor was set down several inches and my feet were soon in water, my clammy toes soaked all over again. I walked until I came to the source of the noise.

I turned on the flashlight.

The noise was generated by a small electric pump. Two hoses were connected to the pump, one disappearing into the pool of stagnant water at my feet, and the other running up through a high window that must have led outside. It was a sump pump to rid the aged leaky crypt of water.

The pump was not significant in any particular way to events at the villa, but its being on meant that the electricity had been restored. I hadn't realized it when the pump first came on, but it now occurred to me that the humming had been going on for at least half an hour. I hastily made my way upstairs and left the church.

A fog had formed in the valley, and it seemed to be

making its way up the mountain. I started back for the
villa, a quickness in my step, a modicum of confidence in
my gray matter. It was dark and cool but the sun would
be up in a few hours and our nightmare would then be
over. I planned how I would approach the *dottore,* and
how with the aid of Cavalliere we would subdue Borromini until the police could arrive. I reached the fork in
the road and turned east for the long climb back to Villa
Piruzzi. It was too foggy to tell if Salò was still dark, but
since the electricity had been on at the little church, then
more than likely it would be back on at the villa. I has-
tened my step and soon thereafter saw the villa gates. But
beyond them the villa was still shrouded in dark.

Then something occurred to me.

Somewhere in the course of my life I've seen images of
the damage violent thunderstorms can do, and what happens when a power line is severed. It is an explosion of
spewing sparks and smoke, with the power line making
wild, snake-like writhings—and it is more than evident to
the human eye. What I now considered was that the
electricity was on at the church, and indeed had been for
some time, and yet as I peered before me, the villa was
still dark. I remembered Piruzzi saying something about
one of the power lines being severed on the mountain. If
power was on at the church and off at the villa, then
somewhere between the two, the power had to be cut.
The power lines paralleled the road I was on. And yet, I
saw no evidence of a severed line. I paused. The fog
wafted at my back. A hard lump rose in my throat, and
I came to another realization.

The electricity at the villa had not been severed by the
storm. The villa was dark, but not because of a power
outage. The villa was dark because someone wanted it
dark. That someone was Borromini. The son of a bitch
had covered every angle. By making it appear that the
power was out, he had kept us at the villa. By making
sure the phones were out, we had no way to reach the
police.

I started forward again. My feet were numb and my knees ached, like they always do when it rains. The outline of the villa came into focus, now enveloped by the fog. My breathing was shallow, but I trotted on. I was drawn by an intangible force, like gravity itself, a force that might mean destruction. I wondered how Keller, Cavalliere and Piruzzi would be dealt with. What would happen to Elena?

I picked up my pace because my fear for them was growing. The flashlight felt like a dead weight in my arm, and my feet like two giant flippers. It was a long climb from the church to the villa, and my body, I'm afraid, was hardly up to it. My thighs were burning and my breath was short, but I had to go on, to do what I could to stop Borromini.

When I reached them, the villa's stone gate piers stood like a pair of ominous sentries, tall and gray, stationary against the mist. I rushed towards them, now running full speed, my breath condensing in the still air like the escaping steam of a runaway locomotive. And suddenly an object lay ahead, a blacker black than the road itself, but I was moving too fast to avoid it. I stumbled in an attempt to miss it and the flashlight fell before me. I rolled, hitting hard on the left shoulder until my body weight dragged upon the gravel and brought me to a jarring stop. The flashlight continued on, spinning in circles of light, until it finally rolled to a stop.

I sat up. A few yards behind me was an object the size of a man, lying full length across the drive. I picked up the flashlight and brought its beam close to the mass. Illuminated in the light was the ashen face of Franco Cavalliere, wet, and peppered with the fine white stones of the drive. His dark hair lay loosely across his face, and blood seeped from the corner of his forehead. What appeared to be a bullet hole had punctured the left shoulder of his tuxedo jacket, still moist and red. I crawled over to where he lay and put my ear to the back of his chest. He was still breathing. His head lay only a foot or so from one of the stone gate piers. He may have been trying to escape for help, or apprehend Borromini, when Borromini shot him. In the melee he must have run into the gate pier and knocked himself unconscious.

I turned out the light. The heels of my hands were burning and raw from my fall. My shirt was ripped and still wet from the rain. My breath was short and it raced to catch up with my heartbeat. My ears were ringing, the chugging of my own breath exploding into the dark night air. Had I been in a safe warm room somewhere, I would have considered my condition pathetic.

I then focused my senses and looked around me, confirming that Borromini was not still here. I rose and lifted Cavalliere's enormous frame. With significant effort I half-carried and half-dragged him down the drive. At the forecourt to the house I took a left and quietly—or as quietly as is possible when dragging a two-hundred-pound body—made my way to the north courtyard. When I was sure that we had not been heard, I moved across the courtyard and carried Cavalliere into Elena's suite of rooms.

Once inside we were assailed by the chirping of her birds. I quickly pulled the door to behind us. That done, I sat Cavalliere on the sofa, removed his jacket and shirt, then lay him gently backwards into the soft leather upholstery. I checked one of Elena's telephones on the off chance that it was working, but of course it was dead.

I then turned on the flashlight and examined Cavalliere's wound. It was just above the elbow of his left arm, in the lower part of his sizable biceps. The bullet appeared to have entered from the rear and had made a fairly clean exit. The blood had coagulated into a thick ooze, and it seeped slowly from both openings. On his forehead was a gash about two inches long, and it too was bleeding slowly. I hastily retrieved a bowl of warm water and some clean dish towels from the kitchen. I worked at cleaning his wounds with gentle speed, then fashioned a bandage wrap of sorts with one of the dish towels. I then found a bottle of Pernod in a cabinet, which I left on the coffee table beside him. That's what they did in the movies.

Leaving him the flashlight, I then hurried back out to the courtyard and silently made my way back to the motor court. My eyes found electrical wires suspended overhead in the fog, and I followed them around the north side of the villa until they turned down the side of the building. A few yards ahead the wires swung over to a pair of conduits mounted on an outside building wall, and there the conduits dropped to the basement. One of the conduits was of a large diameter, which would have been the villa's electrical service. The other was smaller, and I suspected it was for the telephone.

I then searched for a way into the basement along the north wall. There was none, so I returned to the courtyard off of which Elena's rooms opened, and made my way over to a service door that led to the back hall near the villa's kitchen. I had to find the telephone panel, in order to attempt to reconnect the phones.

I opened the door and slithered into the back hall. At the far end of the corridor, where a closed door connected to the dining room, I could see a faint line of light at the door's bottom edge. Beyond that door, and on the other side of the dining room was the candlelit library, and more than likely that's where Borromini had the others. I groped in the darkness for the stairs Paolo Liserio had taken me down when we went to the wine cellar. I found them and descended, into a black abyss. I realized now that I shouldn't have left my flashlight with Cavalliere, but there was no time to waste, so I continued on.

At the bottom of the stairs I felt my way along the basement corridor, moving north to where I knew the electrical service came in. Following the corridor to its end, I located what I thought to be the wine cellar door, because it was locked. I thought that the electrical service must be in a room near the wine cellar, so I found the nearest open door and made my way inside. It was a large room with a pair of high windows at its opposite end. The windows opened to the exterior, and they brought in enough light to lead me to the north wall. Feeling my way along the bumpy surface of the cool rubble foundation wall, I soon came to a pair of metal panels. My hands recognized them as electrical circuit panels. I opened one and fingered my way up to a double circuit breaker. I opened the other and did the same. I suspected that one of the pairs of double breakers would restore the villa's power.

But it wasn't electrical power that I wanted to restore. I continued to search along the north wall for the telephone panel. I wasn't sure what an Italian phone panel looked like, or for that matter what one *felt* like, but it would probably be smaller than the two electrical panels. I knew that the phone service came in via a conduit adjacent to the electrical lead. The panel had to be near me. But I couldn't find it.

I leaned against the wall. My shoulder ached and I was tired. I could hardly remember what day it was, or how long I had even been at the villa. Suddenly I let out a spurt of laughter, thinking about the situation. There were four people upstairs, who though they didn't know it, had one hope in this nightmare. Me. Pretty ridiculous. Some kind of hero I was. In the time I'd wasted groping around the villa, I could have gone straight from the little church down the mountain to Salò. I could have roused Anghini and his men and we could have been back here already, and the revulsion of this night would have been over. But instead I was standing in a dark cold cellar, with my nose running and my shoulder probably sprained, an out-of-shape associate professor of architecture, somebody whose brain probably contained more trivial arcana about Pietro da Cortona or Louis I. Kahn than anyone in the world, but without a goddamned clue as to how to get out of this predicament.

I could only think of one course of action now, but I

considered it carefully, because it was something I might regret. It seemed to me that the only way I was going to find the telephone panel was to turn on the lights. And the only way I was going to turn on the lights would be if I restored power to the villa. By turning on the power, though, I would be telling Borromini where I was.

But I had no choice.

I leaned over to the electrical panels, and taking a deep breath, I flipped one of the double circuit breakers. Nothing dramatic happened, no surge or hum, no sparks—not even lights. I did now notice, though, that across the room, out the corridor door, that the corridor was lit. This jarred me, and I rushed to the far wall and found my own room's light switch. I quickly flipped it on and returned my gaze to the north wall. I immediately saw the penetration of the foundation wall by the phone conduit and I followed it with my eyes down the wall, where it ended about seven feet above the stone floor. No wonder I hadn't found the phone panel. As I could now see, the line had been ripped from the wall.

I thought momentarily about trying to reconnect the line, but within an instant I heard a noise from the other end of the corridor, coming from above. A door was being opened, the door from the upstairs back hall to the cellar stairs. For sure it was Borromini.

I instinctively started for the corridor, but by the time I got there I realized that it only led back to the stairs. I couldn't recall seeing any other way out of the cellar, so I dashed across the corridor into another open doorway, just as I heard his rapid footsteps cascading down the steps. The room I was now in was as dark as the mechanical room, again with two high windows. Footsteps echoed down the winding corridor, and I dashed towards the outer wall. I found some boxes there which I dragged to one of the windows, and luckily the window was unlocked. My breathing was loud. I shimmied up into the narrow opening, glancing back just in time to see him pass and disappear across the corridor. I held my breath.

"Ramsgill, is that you?"

Borromini's voice resonated in the hard vacuous chamber of the mechanical room, expanding outward like the voice of an opera tenor trailing off in a great concert hall. I pulled myself through the open window just as I heard him return to the corridor. He was moving quickly, nothing like the erudite architect who had earlier gained my admiration, but with the frantic desperation of a killer. I couldn't tell if I'd been seen. I gently returned the window to its closed position, then rose to my feet.

I found myself in a deep areaway, a narrow pit lined by the multistoried building wall on one side and a battered stone wall topped by a wrought iron fence on the other. The ground was well above me. Looking up into the misty fog, the distant light of the villa's motor court shone beyond the fence. I briskly walked the length of the areaway searching for a way out. At its south end I reached a dead end. I turned around and hurried north. At the extreme north end of the areaway it veered right, and I continued to walk its narrow path until it began to incline. I was moving downhill now, and to my left, over the wrought iron fence I could sense the woods behind the villa. I was turned once more, again to the right, and now the wall to my left began to disappear. Another twenty yards took me to the ground behind the villa. The areaway ended. I was on a cushion of earth.

I paused for a moment and assured myself that Borromini had not followed me into the areaway. I then started forward along a dark path that paralleled the villa's back wall. The fragrance of evergreens filled the wet air, and the pine needles beneath my feet absorbed all my sound. A few moments later I arrived at the steep steps that rose to the garden of the seven pavilions. I climbed out of the woods and onto the wet granite Belgian block of the garden, just as I thought I heard the distant click of a door being closed. The sound seemed to come from my left, but in the fog, it was hard to get my bearings. I could see the dim light of the dining room, just to my right. To my left I sensed the garden with its empty pavilions. The fog blanketed everything, and it brought to the garden a surrealism, transforming its architectonic structure into a velvet dream. I realized that the one thing I had going for me was the fog. As long as I remained outside, I would be concealed, and since I didn't have a gun, it would put me on more even ground with Borromini.

But I needed something—I couldn't face him empty-handed. Then I remembered there were some kitchen knives in my pavilion, and though a knife is no match for a revolver, at least it was something. Perhaps if I could surprise him in the fog I might have a chance.

I slipped quietly beneath the colonnade that connected the pavilions on the east side of the garden, heading towards its end. I passed Sir Colin's pavilion, then Borromini's own. Halfway between Borromini's pavilion and Thornburgh Keller's, I stopped.

What if he was waiting for me in my pavilion? Was it the sound of my own door that I had heard?

I had no idea where he was. I tried to put myself in his shoes, wondering where he would wait. He could be anywhere. In fact, like in a giant shell game, he could be in any one of the seven pavilions. I turned and started back towards the main house. I had to know if he was lying in wait, but I sure as hell wasn't going to knock on my door. I moved silently back down the colonnade until once again I reached Sir Colin's pavilion. I quietly opened his door.

It was dead silent inside, as if the fog had drifted in and been absorbed by the plaster walls. I climbed the stairs to Garbutt's lightless studio, then made my way to the front window. I silently lifted the sash. I paused for a moment, then crept across the dark studio to the area of his kitchen where I fumbled through some drawers there until I found a knife. It was a paring knife, sharp and short, and though I would have preferred something bigger, it would have to do. Returning to the studio, I then combed the top of the drafting table and found a marble paperweight that would serve my purpose well.

Back at the open window, I stood silent for a few minutes, making sure that no one was lurking beneath me in the mist. I picked my own pavilion out of the haze, and standing back from the window at an angle that would give me a clear shot to my front door, I reared back and threw the paperweight with all the strength I could muster. It bounced once on the wet pavement and caromed up to the door, hitting it broadside waist high. The sound it made in the damp air was like an explosion, and it was followed by two smaller explosions, blasts of gunfire that came from within my pavilion. I next heard the patter of running feet. My door swung open violently and someone stepped outside.

"Ramsgill!"

It was Borromini's voice, a pistol extended in his arm.

"Ramsgill!" he called again, turning from side to side. "Is that you?"

He waited for a response.

"Come out!" he called again. "Where are you?"

He walked out to the area of the bosk and looked about him. From my vantage point he was only twenty or so yards away. He couldn't see me, though, as the fog was thick and soupy.

"Ramsgill! You've got to come inside!" he said. "Cavalliere's out here somewhere and he's got a gun! It was Cavalliere! You were right!"

He waited for a response. I stood as still as a tree.

He paused and cocked an ear to the foggy air. He proceeded with tentative steps to circuit the garden, ending at an overlook on the far side. I didn't know how many shots he had remaining, but I thought I would try to coax some more bullets from the gun.

I found an empty glass in Garbutt's studio and returned to the window. I slid it up higher, to a point where the bottom sash was even with the top sash, leaving a wide opening, large enough to jump from. The opening was only about six feet above the floor, however, and in order to get the glass across the garden I would have to improvise.

I stepped back from the window the length of five paces. I then started forward, and as I came upon the opening I let the glass fly, tossing it sidearm so that it would have enough arc to break when it hit the pavement. I had hardly made a sound, and when it shattered across the way, Borromini practically collapsed. It had so caught him by surprise, however, that he only managed to get off one shot. He must have then realized it wasn't a human sound he was hearing.

This time he didn't call out to me, though it must have been evident to him that I was nearby. He examined the glass shards that surrounded him and then, though it was hard to tell, he seemed to look in my direction. I pressed my sore shoulder against the wall. He started in slow deliberate steps towards me, seeming to realize that the glass's flight had started here. I slid beneath the wall and ducked under the windowsill. I tried to remember if I had closed Garbutt's front door. If it was open, then he was sure to come inside.

His steps continued, reverberating across the empty courtyard, coming closer in a straight line. I fumbled for the knife I had found in Garbutt's kitchen. My fingers caressed the blade, which was only three or four inches long, serrated, but flimsy. I suddenly wondered if it would do the job. I then recalled a letter opener that was in the desk drawer to my pavilion, long and sharp, without a cutting edge, but with a point like a dagger. Maybe Garbutt had one.

The sound of Borromini's footsteps continued and I found myself slithering away from the window, sliding across the wood plank floor. The smell of lemon oil filled my nose. I crawled to Garbutt's desk and reached up into the flat drawer at the kneehole. I fingered the desk supplies there, but I couldn't find the letter opener. I checked one of the side drawers and still didn't find it, but just as

Borromini was arriving outside, I found a pair of pointed scissors, longer even than the letter opener. They were cold to the touch, forged of heavy steel, and they had wide handles into which I could put all of the fingers of my left hand. They felt good there.

I pushed myself away from the desk, and like a ship setting out to sea, I headed for the window that was my ocean. It was through that window that I would live or die, no turning back, no reconsideration of my plan. I wasn't going to sit and wait in the studio for Borromini. I was going to attack.

I tried again to remember if I had left the door open, but now, as I had reformulated my plan, I hoped I had, because if he came for the door, it would bring him just below my window. His pace was slowing now, and I took my spot just under the windowsill. The scissors were clutched tightly in my grasp. I sat perfectly still, my ear cocked to the open window, as he arrived in front of the pavilion. I heard the sound of his last footstep, and then silence as he prepared to pounce.

Then I heard another sound, this one coming from the side of the pavilion, in the recesses under the colonnade. I recognized it again as the hiss of a peacock, and I slowly lifted my eyes above the sill. Borromini stood directly below the window, his gun raised towards the bird. He took one step forward. The bird moved. Borromini jabbed at the air with his gun, started to speak, and then fired. He got off two rounds. The bird screeched and came towards him and again he fired. The peacock went into convulsions and jerked its body spasmodically across the garden towards its center. Halfway to the bosk of olive trees, it became silent.

Borromini's chest heaved for breath. I realized he had just spent his last shell and he seemed to be pulling more bullets from his pocket. I couldn't let him reload.

I raised my foot to the windowsill, grasped the jamb, and held the scissors before me. Suddenly, he looked up, and like a frightened deer frozen by the headlights of an oncoming car, he caught sight of my silhouette in the second-story window. He began scrambling backwards. I stepped from the window and floated downward, much faster and with more force than I could have ever imagined. I was heading towards his wide white eyes, my scissors aimed for his chest, a chest that, though it wasn't large, appeared in my own frightened pupils like a bull's-eye, a huge target into which I would drive my weapon. Then just as suddenly as I had stepped away from the window, a cloud of smoke appeared from the end of his gun, a perfect cloud, like someone exhaling long and hard on a cigar, and then a burning sensation in my leg, like a hot poker passing right through me. But I kept coming and the gun went off again, this time ricocheting on the wall of the pavilion behind me. Our bodies collided, like a hammer hitting an anvil, his legs buckling beneath my weight. His mass cushioned my fall, until the point of my scissors entered his ribcage and I felt the implosion of his lung. We collapsed together to the garden floor, his head striking the pavement with a thud that made me cringe. The force of the landing shook every bone in my body. I strained to maintain consciousness. My head began bobbing and I felt a sudden wave of electricity rushing through my veins. I was very aware of my breathing, which confirmed that I was still alive.

I lifted my head just long enough to gaze into his eyes. They were cold and gray, impressed with the look of fear and death. I felt a rush of nausea coming on, but I couldn't throw up. Then, like a camera shutter stuck from lack of lubrication, my eyes hesitatingly shut. I lost all feeling. It was black.

FIFTEEN

My first sensation after regaining consciousness was a warm wetness at my upper right leg. It was followed almost immediately by pain, a deep pain that pulsated from the top of my forehead all the way down to my feet. My eyes quivered as if they were on tiny springs, and the pungency of torn human flesh filled my nose.

I rolled over and sat up slowly, straining to get my bearings. I was still in the garden, somewhere not far from the olive trees, and it was still night. To my left was a dead peacock, the unfurled feathers of its left wing jackknifed against its white body. From somewhere I heard a slurping sound, and I looked back to Borromini on the ground next to me. The slurping was coming from his chest. A pair of large scissor handles stood erect in the middle of his sternum. I leaned over, shut my eyes and reached for the handles. I grasp them and pulled, lifting upward against the friction of steel upon bone. Blood seemed to bubble from his breastbone.

With the scissors free I then cut away some of the fabric surrounding my own injury. Crimson blood seeped slowly from the wound, gathering into a small puddle on the ground. The wound was on the upper part of my right thigh, and at least the bullet had not shattered bone. I removed my belt and fashioned a crude tourniquet, tying it securely around my leg just above the wound, but not so tight as to cut off circulation.

"Jamie, is that you?"

I looked over stunned to Borromini, who somehow, with a four-inch-deep hole in his chest, had managed to communicate. His voice was sedate and he spoke as if nothing had ever happened between us, as if we were the closest of friends. I slid over to him the best I could and lifted his head, gently placing it upon my good leg.

"It's me," I said. It was too late to be antagonistic. He was dying.

"What happened?" he said. "Why am I bleeding?"

"You're hurt, Gio. Shut your eyes. Relax."

He inhaled a heaving gurgling breath.

"Did I shoot you, Jamie?"

"Yes."

"Sorry," he said.

The way he spoke, it was as if he had just bumped into me on a sidewalk. I didn't respond. I was staring in disbelief at the hole in my leg.

"No, really, I am."

"Why'd you do it, Gio?"

"I wanted the Vitruvius to remain in Italy."

"Mmh," I muttered. A perfectly logical reason to murder five people, I thought.

"You don't understand. Piruzzi had no right to offer it as a prize. I was going to take the manuscript and return it to the Forum in Rome, where it belongs. *Urbi et orbi . . .*"

He halted in mid-sentence as his breathing became more coarse, and he suddenly winced in pain. His eyes fluttered several times before closing. Then his head jerked up.

"Relax," I said, gently guiding his head back to my lap.

"To the city, to the world," he started again, now somewhat delirious. "Don't you realize its importance? It's the history of Roman architecture in all its glory. I thought I would bury it in the ruins . . . in the temple of

Antoninus and Faustina, under the cella floor, along the Via Sacra. Do you think that would have been a good idea?"

"Yes, Gio. It would have been a good idea."

"Jamie, also . . ." his voice was choked up. "I didn't kill Richard . . . I just picked up on the seven sacraments after hearing how Battle died . . . I'm sorry about . . ."

"What? What, Gio?"

His mouth clamped shut and he started struggling to breathe through his nose. He looked as if he were about to throw up. Suddenly he said:

"Could I . . . could I see the manuscript once more?"

He spoke with his eyes still shut. I didn't know how he was going to see anything. I also didn't think that he would live long enough for me to return with the book. There was now blood trickling from the corner of his mouth.

"Let me get you a doctor, Gio."

"No. Please, please get me the Vitruvius."

His voice was resolute, even in its frailty.

"All right," I said.

I removed his head from my lap and rose. A lightheadedness overcame me, and I paused for a moment to steady myself, prior to starting for the house. I had taken but a few tentative steps when I paused again, this time to retrieve his gun, which he still grasped in the tightly wrapped fingers of his left hand. I returned to him and removed it. He might be dying, but it wasn't lost on me that just moments before he had tried to kill me.

I held it out and examined it. It was a small revolver, nickel-plated with a white plastic handle. I guess I had expected something more substantial, more criminal-like, I suppose, but upon reflection, it was in reality the type of gun someone not used to guns might own. The chamber was open, and scattered about on the ground were several spent shells. There were also two live shells on the ground, and I picked them up and loaded them into the chamber.

I then limped up towards the house. When I reached the living room I found Elena, Renzo and Keller all bound together against the long wall opposite the fireplace. I quickly untied them, whereupon they heaved a collective sigh of relief.

"Jamie," said Piruzzi. "So good to see you, son. Where's Borromini and Clissac? And what happened to Franco?"

"Franco's okay," I replied. "Clissac's dead. Borromini's in the garden . . . dying."

"Justice served," said Keller. His face was still white and his clothes a jumbled mess.

"Jamie, your leg," said Elena.

"I was shot," I said. "Listen, we've got to get a doctor."

"I'll get the car keys," said Piruzzi.

He vanished into the front hall, and I limped in some pain over to the vitrine that held the *De architectura* manuscript. I raised the glass and set it aside, then lifted the box that held the manuscript.

"What are you doing with that?" asked Keller.

"Borromini wants to see it," I said.

"Don't you think you ought to ask my permission first?"

I looked at him, incredulous.

"What?"

"I believe that since I'm the only remaining architect in the competition, the manuscript now belongs to me."

I studied his face, which was full of apprehension.

"Go to hell, Keller. Besides, Borromini's not dead yet. And given the circumstances, you don't think Piruzzi's still going to give away the book, do you?"

He shuffled across the floor to a point just out of my reach and stared up at me. His eyes were like pots of boiling liquid. He looked as though he had been out on an all-night drunk.

"You're goddamned right I think he's going to give it

up. He had a verbal contract with us. And he'll honor it
. . . or I'll sue him."

I somehow mustered a laugh. If the elite of the architecture world could only see Keller as I was seeing him
now, whimpering in his stocking feet, still trying to get
his money-grubbing hands on the manuscript.

"You're too much," I said.

"Here we are," said Piruzzi, re-entering the room from
the front hall. "We can go now."

I stared at Keller until he backed away.

"Good," I said. I turned and motioned Elena ahead of
me, towards the door. Piruzzi and Keller followed us out.
I carried the manuscript in one hand and Borromini's
revolver in the other.

As we stepped down from the dining terrace and into
the garden, I surveyed the foggy world before us. The
horizon to the east was just beginning to warm, and with
the coming of daylight, the seven pavilions of the garden
were etched by fog. It was as though we had stepped into
a sunrise painted by Georges Seurat. Diminutive dots of
pointillist pastel—orange, pink and gray—composed the
scene, all fused together by the indeterminate vapor. The
dark crowns of the olive trees stood out gray against the
pastel mist, and midway up the garden Borromini lay
dying.

We came upon the sound of his strained breathing,
and I knelt beside him with the manuscript box in my
hand. I lay the revolver on the ground and proceeded to
remove the manuscript.

"Here it is, Gio."

His hands levitated above his chest and swung like the
hands of a marionette over to where I was kneeling. They
made contact with the ancient parchment, and we
watched as he tenderly felt the ripples and torn edges of
the paper.

"Beautiful . . . yes?"

His voice was weak, and I now knew, even as I suspected earlier, that he would never survive a trip down the mountain to a hospital.

"May I?" he asked. His eyelids were still closed, but he now had a full grasp upon the pieces of parchment and was lifting them from my hands. He pulled them closer to his bleeding breast.

"Stop!" snapped Thornburgh Keller, standing to my left. "You're not going to let him ruin it by bleeding all over it, are you?"

Borromini's hands halted their motion. His face showed pain.

"Get it away from him," Keller demanded.

"Who's that?" Borromini asked, his voice fading as if he were under the effects of a sedative.

"It's Thornburgh," I said. "Maybe he's right, Gio. Why don't I just hold the manuscript for you."

He continued to clutch the papers. I didn't want to upset him, but I sure as hell wasn't going to let him ruin such an important document.

"Okay," he finally said weakly. "I won't . . . if Piruzzi agrees . . ."

I looked to Piruzzi.

"If I agree to what?" he said.

Borromini took a long horrible breath.

"Agree that . . . Vitruvius . . . stays in Italy."

Piruzzi's broad hands reached over and grasped the other end of the manuscript.

"All right," he said. "I do."

Borromini slowly released the pages.

"Finito," he said.

I took the manuscript from Piruzzi and carefully returned it to its temple box. With a single finger I slowly hinged the top shut.

Borromini seemed to signal his approval by the slightest smile. He then brought his feeble hands up to his chest and crossed them over his bloody wound. A blank stare drifted over his face like a shroud. He said nothing more.

We watched in silence, and waited, as he slowly slipped away.

It took several more long minutes for him to die.

"We should cover him up," said Piruzzi, once it was clear he was gone. "I'll pull the car around."

"Okay," I said, rising with the manuscript box.

I turned and put my free hand on Elena's shoulder. She responded by wrapping her long arms around my neck.

"It's over," I whispered.

She pulled my bruised forehead towards her until it met her delicate lips. She then kissed it lightly, like a mother making a child's scratch go away. I glanced over at the *dottore,* expecting him to give me a look of disapproval. This time, he smiled.

"Just a minute," said Thornburgh Keller, standing behind us, intruding upon the scene.

I looked up. Keller was on the other side of Borromini's body, a few yards away. I was about to tell him where I thought he could go, when, as I looked down to his hands, I could see that he was holding Borromini's revolver. Or pointing it, rather. In our direction.

"Don't be ridiculous," Piruzzi said. "Put down the gun before you hurt somebody."

"No," he said, with trepidation in his voice. "It's mine."

"Oh yeah," I said as I pulled away from Elena. "Thornburgh's claiming the manuscript, Renzo."

With my free hand I touched Elena's waist and guided her to a point behind me, putting myself between her and Keller's gun. The gun was shaking, and my worst fear was that it would go off accidentally.

"I heard you tell Borromini that you would keep the manuscript in Italy," Keller said, his voice rising. "But it's mine. I've won the competition. I've outlasted them all!"

I think that in a delusional sort of way, he actually thought he had won. He seemed buoyed by this fact, and all of a sudden his face exhibited an expression that was somewhere between nervous joy and madness. His face was still white, and the pistol continued to waver in his feeble hands. His eyes now appeared to be looking right through us, as if he were seeing on a different plane.

"There was no end to the competition," Piruzzi said. "There *is* no winner."

"But, you can't renege," Keller said. "I'm within my rights."

"I'm afraid not, my friend."

Keller stared silently at our host.

"I . . . I should shoot you," he said. "But I won't."

Instead he turned to me.

"Now, give me the manuscript."

"Keller, this is absurd. I think—"

"I could care less what you think," he interjected. "Just give me the manuscript."

I stepped forward and held out the box. He grasped it tentatively with his free hand, but I didn't let go. I knew that he had two bullets left in the gun. I had no idea if he was capable of firing them, or much less of hitting anyone. But in the state he was in, it was clear to me that he might try.

"Let go," he said, almost pleading.

I tightened my grip. He scowled and his breathing escalated.

"Jamie," Elena finally said.

I continued to stare down at him. There was no point in being a hero, however, especially a dead one. He didn't have any realistic chance of escaping, anyway. I tugged once at the box and then shoved it back at his chest.

"Don't do this," Piruzzi said, once Keller had possession of the box. "You're not a common criminal."

I considered that statement carefully. Something Borromini had said came to mind, and before I could think about it, I spoke.

"But he is," I said.

Keller turned to me, fire in his eyes.

"He killed Richard Battle," I said. "I wouldn't call him a *common* criminal, but he's a murderer just the same."

"Why do you say this, Jamie?" asked Piruzzi, stepping to a point behind Elena and me. "I thought Borromini was the murderer."

"He was," I said. "Of the others. But he told me that he didn't kill Richard. I didn't think about it earlier, but now it makes sense."

"What?" asked Piruzzi.

"Borromini killed the others to keep the Vitruvius manuscript from leaving Italy, as he said, but Richard was killed the night *before* you unveiled the manuscript to us. Unless of course you had already told Borromini about the manuscript."

"No, no. The manuscript was a secret. No one but Franco knew about it prior to the morning I showed it to you all."

"Then Richard was killed for another reason," I said. "Which means he was killed by someone else."

"But how do you know it was Keller?"

"I don't . . . for sure."

I looked into Keller's angry eyes.

"You told me on Sunday that you would do anything, *anything* to win the competition. And you thought that Richard was the man to beat. It certainly wouldn't have hurt your chances in the competition if the favorite didn't compete, would it?"

He laughed an edgy laugh. "No, it wouldn't. Does that mean I killed him? Where's your proof?"

"I don't have any really, except that Borromini certainly knew enough not to substitute a Chianti for a Recioto in Richard's glass. Only someone who didn't know Italian wines would do that. I remember that when we first tasted the Recioto in the library after dinner, you asked Cavalliere if it was Chianti we were drinking."

"So you say."

"Also," I continued. "Cavalliere told us that he never

took a Chianti from the wine cellar. You could have easily forged his initials to frame him."

"But the wine cellar's always locked," said Piruzzi. "If as you are suggesting, Keller took the Chianti from the cellar, then how did he get in?"

"He didn't need to," I said.

"What?"

"He didn't need to. I didn't say that the Chianti *actually* came from the cellar. Maybe it did, maybe it didn't. All Keller had to do was to make it *appear* that Cavalliere had logged out the wine. And the wine log is not in the cellar. It hangs on a hook out in the basement corridor. Anyone could have gotten to it and forged Cavalliere's initials."

"Very good," Keller said, once I had finished. "Maybe you'll get your tenure yet, Ramsgill. Sorry I won't be able to put in a good word for you, though. I'm afraid I must be going."

He clutched the manuscript box as if it were a baby.

"You'll never get away, my friend," Piruzzi said. "The authorities will be on to you before you get out of Salò."

Keller pondered for a moment before speaking.

"Will they?" he said, his eyes darting. "Then maybe I'll ask your daughter to join me. My insurance, as it were."

Elena stepped up close to my back.

"No way," I said. "Take me if you want someone."

"No, that won't do. You're just another foreigner as far as the police are concerned. She, on the other hand, is the daughter of this country's richest citizen."

I hooked her waist with the palm of my left hand. She clutched my fingers with a tight grip and dug her chin into my back.

"Enough of this," Keller said. "Hand her over, now, or I'll shoot."

He raised the barrel of the revolver and pointed it towards my good leg. He then waited for a response, but when he didn't get one, he slowly raised the gun from my leg and pointed it at my head. It was shaking wildly now.

"Basta!" Elena said abruptly, pulling away from me and jumping over to Keller before I could stop her.

"That's better," he said. "And I want those car keys, too, Renzo."

Piruzzi reluctantly handed over the keys. Keller gave Elena the box, and with his free hand, grabbed her arm.

"Let her go, Keller. As the *dottore* says, you'll never get out of Salò. And even if you do, where will you go? You're finished. Just like your career, you're finished."

He tightened his grip on Elena's arm.

"Sorry to disappoint you," he said. "But we're going. And you won't try to follow us . . . will you?"

He didn't expect an answer, I suppose, and we didn't give him one. He gave Elena a nudge with the gun barrel, and she reluctantly started forward. As she did so she gazed over to me, her eyes filled with fear. I started to speak, but nothing came out.

Piruzzi and I then watched helplessly as the two of them stepped away and evaporated into the fog. We stood there silently, neither of us knowing what to do. I felt helpless, and ridiculous for letting Keller get away with this.

But the feeling didn't last long.

Only a few seconds later we heard a gunshot, coming from up near the drive. It was a single sharp pop, and the sound darted through the air like a sparrow.

I leapt forward. Racing across the garden I took the stairs up to the forecourt three risers at a time. At the top I rounded the villa and jumped the curb onto the drive. I could see the faint outline of three bodies sprawled out before me on the wet pavement, lit by the rising sun. Two of the bodies watched the third as it writhed in excruciating pain. Its head was tucked into its knees, moaning, and then it became still. I heard the clink of metal on pavement.

"Elena?" I said. In the fog I couldn't tell who was who.

"Yes?" she replied. I connected the voice to a figure that was just now rising from the pavement. She then took the hand of the third figure. It was then that I realized, even in the fog, that the large frame of the third figure belonged to Franco Cavalliere.

"Thank God," I muttered.

Renzo Piruzzi walked up behind me.

"Thank God, indeed," he said.

EPILOGUE

Venice, August 13

Almost a week has passed since I left the Villa Piruzzi, and as I write this, I gaze out from beneath my hotel room terrace, beyond the Riva degli Schiavoni, and onto the sublime and majestic Canale di San Marco. Vaporetti chug steadily across the broad water toward the Giudecca, entwining with the glossy black gondolas that bob like seesaws in the turbulence of their wake. Gulls circle and glide in the cerulean sky, and tourists stroll along the broad curve of the quay. Across the glistening water, San Giorgio Maggiore radiates white in the brilliance of the morning sun, flanked by the ebullient Santa Maria della Salute and the Dogana di Mare.

I can't describe how I feel to be in this place, my health improving by the day, my spirits exalted by the simple fact that I'm still alive. I have a deep sympathy for my colleagues who died, but after pondering for days what I could have done, or what I should have done earlier, I've finally arrived at a personal peace. I now know that none of us could have predicted what transpired at Piruzzi's villa, and even if we could, it wouldn't necessarily have changed things. And I can take some consolation in the fact that I alone stopped Borromini before he could complete his carnage.

I must admit that Piruzzi has more than shown his gratitude for my efforts. It began the day after our ordeal ended. I was in the Salò hospital, a dinosaur of a Modernist building from the Fascist era, one of those cool rational structures that always look better in drawings than they ever do in real life. I occupied a dark second-floor room that overlooked a loading dock, just steps away from Cavalliere's own room. There was nothing to look at but the four walls and two oversized fluorescent lights above my head, until at least an army of Piruzzi's servants brought a multitude of flowers to my room, all sent to me by my former host. The wound to my leg was healing nicely, and from that point on the worst I could say about my condition was that my late-summer allergies were reacting rather badly to the profusion of blooms.

"Ramsgill!" Piruzzi chirped as he entered my room that day. "How are you?"

"Not bad," I said softly. Though my leg was undoubtedly better, my head was still sore, and speaking at any reasonable decibel level sent pain down my jaw.

His black eyes shifted around the small room, within which almost every surface was covered by his floral largesse.

"I do hope you like flowers," he said as he smoothed his thick moustache with pudgy fingers.

I nodded agreeably, making no mention of my allergies.

"Jamie, I must thank you for what you did. If it weren't for you we might not be here today. And to show you my gratitude, I've brought you a little something."

He had been holding an arm behind his rather large mid-section. From it he produced the familiar temple-like box that had held the Vitruvius manuscript. He held it out in my direction.

"I want you to have this," he said.

"The box?" I asked.

"The box *cum* manuscript," he replied.

I studied his face to see if I sensed a joke at work there.

He raised his eyebrows and tipped the box again in my direction. It wasn't a joke.

When I was sure he was serious, I reached out and accepted it. I lightly touched my fingers to the inlaid wood and ran them over the contours of the box like a blind person reading braille. I then slid aside the door that revealed the button that opened the box, and pushed it.

The lid eased open, revealing the priceless contents within.

"I don't think so," I said with a laugh, thumbing through the pages with care.

He eyed me with astonishment.

"Don't look at me like that," I said. "You'll only make me feel more a fool than I already do."

"Jamie, my son, do you know what you're turning down?"

Unfortunately, I did. But it wasn't right. No matter how attractive it seemed, the thought of me owning such an artifact simply didn't wash. It belonged in a library, or in a museum.

"I agree with Borromini, Renzo. The manuscript should be Italy's. If you're willing to give it to me, then why not donate it to the *Gabinetto Nazionale* in Rome? Make it a condition of your gift that it never be sold or allowed to leave the country. Besides . . . you promised Borromini."

He considered my words. I seemed to sense a genuine admiration in his jewel-like eyes.

"You're a good man, my friend," he said. "I don't consider a promise to Borromini worth anything, but I'll do as you say."

I nodded.

"I still want to show you my appreciation," he said a moment later. "What can I do for you?"

I contemplated what one of the world's wealthiest men could offer me, a young teacher who basically lived a pretty simple life. My eyes moved to the cold steel window on the opposite wall of my room. Outside, the sky had darkened and it was beginning to rain.

"Okay," I said after refocusing my eyes on Piruzzi. "You can do this. Is your ownership of the Vitruvius still a secret?"

A puzzled look washed over his face, but he then nodded.

"And has anyone outside the circle of architects who were at your villa, or Elena and Cavalliere, seen it?"

"No. With the exception of the person I bought it from. And my insurance company, of course."

"Of course," I said. "But that's okay. I just want to know if you've shown it to any historians."

"No. As I said, its discovery has been kept a secret."

"Then what I would like, Renzo, is for you to give me access to the manuscript for six months or so, before you release it to the *Gabinetto*."

"But of course, Jamie. This is for scholarly purposes, then?"

"Yes."

"Then you must have it."

I thought for a moment before speaking.

"I'll have to return to the States for a few weeks," I said. "But given the circumstances, I'm sure I can arrange a sabbatical from the university. I'll return shortly, and with your permission, I'll come to the villa to translate the manuscript. Six months should give me adequate time to translate and prepare a new edition of *De architectura*. The literary world will no doubt clamor for the opportunity to publish the edition. Casting all humility aside, I think then that I'll be able to ensure my tenure with the school."

"I would be pleased to help you in such an endeavor," Piruzzi said.

I returned the box to his hands for safe keeping.

"By the way," I said. "Where's Elena?"

I hadn't seen her, but my mind had hardly been on anything else for the last twenty-four hours.

"She told me to apologize for the fact that she didn't come," he said. "She's unexpectedly gone to Bologna."

"Bologna?" There was a decidedly disappointed tone to my voice. She and I had never talked to one another about our personal lives. I now wondered, if in all of my daydreams about her, I had simply missed the fact that she was already attached, that perhaps she had someone waiting for her in Bologna. I stared out my window at the barren concrete wall above the loading dock. Big drops of rain now slapped at the wall like paint being splattered over a Jackson Pollock canvas. The raindrops reminded me of tears.

"She has some business with the university there."

My eyes returned to the room.

"What kind of business, if you don't mind my asking?"

"It seems that Elena has talked me into not building my chapel after all," he said. "You know how she is about those silly birds. And not only did I agree not to build the chapel, but also—and I must be going *matto*— I've agreed to donate the villa and its grounds to the school as a study center. She's meeting with university officials today to discuss the project."

I smiled. "You are feeling magnanimous," I said. "First the Vitruvius, now the villa. I might just begin to feel sorry for you."

"No need for that," he said. "I've decided that my money only has meaning in one world, Jamie. This one. If I've learned anything from this past week, it's just that. You can't take it with you."

If I hadn't understood Piruzzi in the beginning, it was probably because he didn't understand himself. There was no doubt in my mind now, however, where he was heading in the future. He was going to enjoy life.

"What'll you do now?" I asked. "Where'll you live?"

"Jamie, you speak of me as if I'm homeless. I still have my palazzo in Milan. And a chalet in Gstaad. And the yacht in Crete. I don't think that I'll lack for a place to lay my head."

"No, I don't think that you will."

It was at this point that a nurse strolled into the room. She was young and attractive, and she smiled at Piruzzi as she passed him. He noticed the smile, and his eyes followed hers as she made her way to my bed. She carried a tray full of medication, which she began to give me, each pill followed by a gulp of water from a paper cup. Once finished, she hastily fluffed up my pillows, then tucked in my covers all around the bed. She then strode for the door, and we watched her exit, Piruzzi's eyes remaining on the doorway until the sound of her heels on the concrete floor could no longer be heard.

He smiled and shook his head, giving me one of those quintessential Italian machismo looks.

He then walked over to a large bowl of flowers on my dresser. After sorting through a number of blossoms, he choose a salmon-colored lily, clipping its top with a moustache trimmer he had pulled from his pocket. He slid the flower neatly into the lapel of his white silk jacket and gave the lapel a pat. He then walked leisurely towards the hall, pausing and turning on a heel of a Gucci loafer to face me once he reached the door. His smile was as wide as the Mediterranean.

He backed out into the hallway, the whole time keeping his eye upon me. When he reached its middle, he bowed.

"I think," he said, "that I have some living left to do."

A knock on my hotel room door woke me from a fitful nap. I looked up startled and realized I was still on the terrace, the sun now well over the Piazza San Marco. It was late afternoon and the sun's glare on the Canale di San Marco set the water afire. The tourist crowds that normally crammed the *piazzetta* fronting the canal had dissipated, the heat no doubt driving them indoors until evening. I wiped a bead of sweat from my forehead. My neck was stiff from sleeping in my chair.

I heard the knock again, this time more forceful and with an impatient rapidity. Muttering some mild profanities I struggled to my unsteady feet and hobbled across the thick carpet towards the door. I was barefoot, and the toes of my good leg dug into the carpet's plushness.

"Yes?" I answered, pressing my nose to the door.

"Room service," said a feminine voice from beyond.

I didn't order room service, I thought. Or did I? I wanted to go back to sleep. I considered for a moment not opening the door, the limpness of my mind telling me something wasn't quite right.

But then I smiled.

I pulled back the door.

"Did you order something, sir?"

My smile burst forth.

"You," I said.

Elena wrapped her tender arms around my stiff neck.

"How'd it go?" I asked.

"Fine," she said. "I can pick up my visa at the consulate tomorrow."

"Then we can leave on Thursday."

"I'm happy," she said.

"Me too."

I pulled her towards the bed.

We didn't go out until late that evening, long after the sun had dropped from the hot orange horizon. The sky was now a black womb, its infiniteness a great vacuum chamber stretching out to the other side of nowhere. Below the black, just above the waters of the canal, festival lights twinkled, as if some ethereal powder had been sprinkled over the harbor. Strands of tiny white lights were draped lazily upon boat masts, and the lines of light rocked to and fro with the gentle rhythm of the waves. People hugged the shoreline to get a glimpse of the regatta, and low muffled voices hung like a cloud over the quay. Elena and I strolled randomly through the crowd, hand in hand, oblivious to the fireworks, until we reached a graceful stone bridge well away from the noise.

She led me to its top, and there we paused, the warm moist air of the lagoon drifting in like the tide. Behind us, the city spread out over the flat sparkling water like an elaborate tea service on an opulent silver tray. Anthropomorphic palazzi stood shoulder to shoulder along the Riva, each a slight variation of its neighbor. Interspersed among the palazzi were the grand hotels and tiny sidewalk cafes, and beyond, the geometric domes of venerable old churches poked above the skyline like tulips in early spring. Spidery antennas topped terra-cotta roofs, and beneath them were simple courtyard houses with television sets that flickered from behind the lace curtains of open balcony doors. Fresh hand-washed laundry was strung across tiny courtyards, and window boxes overflowed with flowers. A faint aria in the distance competed with a dog's bark, both reverberating down the narrow alleys and byways of the medieval town. Bells echoed, and voices faded in and out of range. Water lapped gently at our feet. I took Elena's arm, looked down into her eyes and smiled.

It felt right to be with her, like something that had always been there. The beauty of the moment overwhelmed me, and I realized, just then, that Italy had recaptured my heart.

In prison, they call her the Sculptress for the strange figurines she carves—symbols of the day she hacked her mother and sister to pieces and reassembled them in a blood-drenched jigsaw. Sullen, menacing, grotesquely fat, Olive Martin is burned-out journalist Rosalind Leigh's only hope of getting a new book published.

But as she interviews Olive in her cell, Roz finds flaws in the Sculptress's confession. Is she really guilty as she insists? Drawn into Olive's world of obsessional lies and love, nothing can stop Roz's pursuit of the chilling, convoluted truth. Not the tidy suburbanites who'd rather forget the murders, not a volatile ex-policeman and her own erotic response to him, not an attack on her life.

MINETTE WALTERS
THE SCULPTRESS

"Creepy but compulsive...The assured British stylist doesn't let up on her sensitive probing of two tortured souls...Hard to put down."
—*The New York Times Book Review*

THE SCULPTRESS
Minette Walters
_____95361-5 $4.99 U.S.

THE SARAH DEANE MYSTERIES BY

(❀) **J. S. BORTHWICK** (❀)

FROM ST. MARTIN'S PAPERBACKS
—COLLECT THEM ALL!

BODIES OF WATER
_____ 92603-0 $4.50 U.S./$5.50 Can.

THE CASE OF THE HOOK-BILLED KITES
_____ 92604-9 $4.50 U.S./$5.50 Can.

THE DOWN EAST MURDERS
_____ 92606-5 $4.50 U.S./$5.50 Can.

THE STUDENT BODY
_____ 92605-7 $4.50 U.S./$5.50 Can.

THE BRIDLED GROOM
_____ 95505-7 $4.99 U.S./$5.99 Can.